国家出版基金项目
NATIONAL PUBLICATION FOUNDATION

十二奴局

赵官禄　郭纯礼　黄世荣　梁福生　搜集整理
张立玉　曹盼盼　英译　[美]H. W. Lan 审校

"十三五"国家重点图书
中国南方民间文学典籍英译丛书
丛书主编　张立玉　丛书副主编　起国庆

THE TWELVE HANI SONGS

出品单位：
中南民族大学南方少数民族文库翻译研究基地
云南省少数民族古籍整理出版规划办公室

WUHAN UNIVERSITY PRESS
武汉大学出版社

·汉英对照·

图书在版编目(CIP)数据

十二奴局:汉英对照/赵官禄等搜集整理;张立玉,曹盼盼英译.—武汉:武汉大学出版社,2021.6(2022.1 重印)

中国南方民间文学典籍英译丛书/张立玉主编

“十三五”国家重点图书　2020 年度国家出版基金资助项目

ISBN 978-7-307-21919-9

Ⅰ.十…　Ⅱ.①赵…　②张…　③曹…　Ⅲ.彝族—史诗—云南—汉、英　Ⅳ.I222.7

中国版本图书馆 CIP 数据核字(2020)第 223307 号

责任编辑:谢群英　李晶晶　　责任校对:汪欣怡　　版式设计:韩闻锦

出版发行:**武汉大学出版社**　(430072　武昌　珞珈山)

(电子邮箱:cbs22@ whu.edu.cn　网址:www.wdp.whu.edu.cn)

印刷:湖北恒泰印务有限公司

开本:720×1000　1/16　印张:23.75　字数:285 千字

版次:2021 年 6 月第 1 版　2022 年 1 月第 2 次印刷

ISBN 978-7-307-21919-9　定价:68.00 元

序

近年来，民族典籍英译捷报频传，硕果累累。韩家全教授等人的壮族系列经典翻译陆续出版，王宏印教授等人的系列民族典籍英译研究著作已经问世，李正栓教授等人的藏族格言诗英译著作不断在国内外出版，王维波教授等人的东北民族典籍英译著作纷纷付梓，李昌银教授等人的“云南少数民族经典作品英译文库”于2018年年底出版，其他民族典籍英译作品也在接踵而至。

近日，中南民族大学张立玉教授传来佳音：他们要出版“十三五”国家重点图书——“中国南方民间文学典籍英译丛书”。虽叫民间文学，其实基本上都是民族典籍。这一系列包括十本书，它们是：《黑暗传》《哭嫁歌》《哈尼阿培聪坡坡》《彝族民间故事》《南方民间创世神话选集》《十二奴局》《召树屯》《娥并与桑洛》《金笛》《梅葛》。其中，好几本是云南少数民族的。只有一本是汉族典籍，即《黑暗传》。很有意思的是，这些典籍展示了不同民族的创世史诗或诸如此类的东西。

《黑暗传》以民间歌谣唱本形象地描述了盘古开天辟地结束混沌黑暗，人类起源及社会发展的历程，融合了盘古、女娲、伏羲、炎帝神农氏、黄帝轩辕氏等众多英雄人物在洪荒时代艰难创世的一系列神话传说。它被称为汉族首部创世史诗。《哈尼阿培聪坡坡》是一部完整地记载哈尼族历史沿革的长篇史诗，堪称哈尼族的“史记”，长5000余行，以现实主义手法记叙了哈尼族祖先在各个历史时期的迁徙情况，并对其迁徙各地的原因、路线、途程，各个迁居地的社会生活、生产、风习、宗教，以及与毗邻民族的关系等，均作了详细而生动的辑录，因而该作品不仅具有文学价值，而且具有重大的历史学、社会学及宗教学价值。《南方民间创世神话选集》包括一些创世神话，主要是关于世界起源和人类起源的神话。本书是一部在哈尼族广泛流传的民间诗歌，它通过“哈尼”(传统歌)的形式在民间演唱，世代流传。“奴局”是哈尼语，相当于汉族著述中的“篇”、“章”或汉族曲艺中的曲目。“十二奴局”即十二路歌的意思。译著表现了远古哈尼先民奇特的想象，涉及天体自然、人类发展、哈尼历史、历法计算、四时季令、农事活动等各个方面的知识，完整地反映了哈尼先民对天地形成、人类起源、民族迁徙的认识，具有创世神话与英雄史诗的合集之性质，可以说是哈尼族最为重要的文学经典之一。《梅葛》是彝族的一部长篇史诗，流传在云南省楚雄州的姚安、大姚等彝族地区。“梅葛”本为一种彝族歌调的名称，由于人们采用这种调子来唱彝族的创世史，因而创世史诗被称为“梅葛”。

其余几本书展示了一些少数民族的风俗习惯、恋爱故事、斗争故事等。《哭嫁歌》是土家族文化典籍。“哭嫁”是土家族姑娘在出嫁时进行的一种用歌声来诉说自己在封建买办婚姻制度下不幸命运的活动，指土家族姑娘的抒情歌谣，富有诗韵和乐感，融哀、怨、喜和乐为一体，以婉转的曲调向世人展示土家人独特的“哭”文化。《彝族民间故事》是一部以流传于云南楚雄彝族自治州彝族人民中间的民间故事为主体，同时覆盖全省包括小凉山等彝族地区的民间故事集。这些故事丰富多彩，从中能看到民族民间故事的各种形态和生动、奇妙而颇具彝族民族特色的文化特征。《召树屯》是傣族民间长篇叙事诗，叙述了傣族佛教世俗典籍《贝叶经 · 召树屯》中一个古老的传说故事。这部叙事诗一直为傣族人民所传唱，历久不衰。《娥并与桑洛》是一部优美生动的叙事诗，一个凄美的爱情悲剧。《金笛》是一部苗族长篇叙事诗，富于变幻性和传奇性，尽情铺叙扎董丕冉与蒙诗彩奏的悲欢离合，热情赞颂他们在与魔虎的激烈斗争中所表现出来的坚贞不屈、英勇顽强的精神，许多情节含有浓郁的民族特色。

这些故事都很引人入胜，都很符合国家文化发展需求，向世人讲述中国故事，传播中华文化，并且讲述的是民族故事，充分体现了党和国家对各民族的关怀。

民族典籍英译是传播中国文化、文学和文明的重要途径，是中华文化“走出去”的重要组成部分，是国家战略，是提高文化“软实力”的重要方式，在文化交流和文明建设中起着不可或缺的作用，对提升中国国际话语权和构建中国对外话语体系以及对建设世界文学都有积极意义。

中国民族典籍使世界文化更加丰富多彩、绚丽多姿。我国各民族典籍中折射出的文化多样性极大地丰富了世界多元、特色鲜明的文化。人们对多样性形成全新的认识角度和思维方式，有助于开阔视野，丰富思考问题的角度，挖掘这些经典中的教育价值和文化价值，对世界其他民族都有指导和借鉴意义，并且有助于建设我国的文化自信。

民族典籍翻译与研究事业关乎国家的稳定统一，关乎民族关系的和谐发展，关乎世界多元文化的实现。在中国，民族典籍资源极为丰富，有待进一步挖掘、翻译，仍有许多少数民族典籍亟待拯救，民族典籍翻译与研究工作任重而道远，民族典籍翻译事业大有可为。

李正栓①

2019 年 7 月 19 日

① 李正栓，中国英汉语比较研究会典籍英译专业委员会常务副会长兼秘书长；中国中医药研究促进会传统文化翻译与国际传播专业委员会常务主任委员。

目　录

Contents

一、牡底密底[1]

萨啦阿依[2]——
很古很古的时候，
天地混沌不分，
世间没有宽宽的大地，
世间没有高高的蓝天，
天神没有地方住，
地神没有地方住。

世间没有宽宽的大地，
世间没有高高的蓝天，
天神不会在，
四面八方到处走；
地神不会在，
四面八方到处游。

人种不会生出来，
财种不会生出来，
庄稼不会长出来，

---

① 牡底密底：哈尼语，即开天辟地。
② 萨啦阿依：哈尼族歌手演唱起首的衬词。

Ⅰ. Mudimidi①

Sala'ayi②—
In the very ancient times,
heaven and earth were indistinguishable,
without the wide land
or the high blue sky,
with no place for the god of heaven to live,
or the god of earth to live.

There was not the wide land
or the high blue sky,
so the god of heaven would not
walk around everywhere;
the god of earth would not
wander about everywhere.

Humans could not be born,
nor could money appear,
nor could crops grow,

---

① Mudimidi: creation of heaven and earth in the Hani language.
② Salaayi: Hani singers refrain in the beginning of the song.

万物不会生出来，
不造天不行了，
不造地不行了，

天是哪日造的？
地是哪天造的？
天是属龙的那天造的，
地是属蛇的那天造的①。

造天的是哪个？
造地的是哪个？
造天的是朱比阿龙②，
造地的是朱比拉沙③。

天是怎样造的？
地是怎样造的？
阿龙把天一片一片辟出来，
拉沙把地一块一块开出来。
天劈出来了，
地开出来了。
可是劈出来的天，
高高低低不整齐；

① 哈尼族是采用十二生肖记日法，他们将龙日定为第一日，蛇日是第二日。

② 朱比阿龙：哈尼族传说中造天的神。

③ 朱比拉沙：哈尼族传说中造地的神。

everything would not come into being,
so the heaven had to be created,
and the earth had to be made.

When was the heaven created?
When was the earth made?
The heaven was created on the day of dragon,
and the earth was made on the day of snake①.

Who created the heaven?
Who made the earth?
It was Zhubi Along② who created the heaven,
and it was Zhubi Lasha③ who made the earth.

How was the heaven created?
How was the earth made?
Along excavated the heaven little by little,
Lasha excavated the earth bit by bit.
The heaven was now created,
so was the earth made.
But the heaven created was
uneven;

---

① The Hani uses the Twelve Animal signs (shengxiao) to number days and set the day of dragon as the first day, and the snake as the second day.

② Zhubi Along: the creation god of heaven in Hani legends.

③ Zhubi Lasha: the creation god of earth in Hani legends.

可是开出来的地，
坑坑洼洼不平坦。
轮着耙天啰，
轮着耙地啰。

借来天神的金耙，
借来天神的黄牛，
天头耙三道，
天中耙三道，
天脚耙三道，
把天耙平了。

借来天神的银耙，
借来天神的水牛，
地头耙三道，
地中耙三道，
地脚耙三道，
把地耙平了。

天的四方平滑了，
地的四方平坦了，
可是天和地空空荡荡，
到处是漆黑一团。

他们用金子做成太阳，
用玉石做成月亮，
用银子做成星星，
挂在高高的天上；

and the earth made,
was rugged.
They took turns to rake the heaven
and to rake the earth.

With the borrowed gold rake,
and cattle from the god of heaven,
the top of the heaven was raked three times,
then the middle of it three times,
and the bottom of it three times.
The heaven was then made smooth.

With the borrowed silver rake,
and the water-buffaloes from the god of earth,
the top of the earth was raked three times,
then the middle of it three times,
and the bottom of it three times.
The earth was then made flat.

The four directions of the heaven were now smooth,
and the four sides of the earth was flat,
but heaven and earth were empty,
and were dark everywhere.

They used gold to make the sun,
used jade to make the moon,
used silver to make the stars,
and hanged them up in the high sky.

从此天上有光亮了，
从此地上有光亮了。

莫米①用木梳把太阳光梳下来，
莫米用木梳把月亮光梳下来。
太阳撒下十二道金线，
月亮撒下十二道银线：
一条线照天边，
一条线照地边，
一条线照天和地中间，
一条线照人，
一条线照飞禽，
一条线照走兽，
一条线照河流，
一条线照山冈，
一条线照长谷子的水田，
一条线照长草木的大地，
一条线照栽棉花的河坝，
一条线照栽荞子的高山。
四面八方都照到了，
世间没有照不着的地方了。

云雾是怎样来的？
山风是怎样来的？
天上的雷声是怎样来的？
天边的闪电是怎样来的？

---

① 莫米：哈尼族传说中的天神。

From then on, there was light in the heaven
and there was light on the earth.

Momi① combed the sunlight down with a wooden comb,
and combed the moonlight down with a wooden comb.
The sun cast down twelve golden threads,
and the moon, twelve silver threads:
one on the heaven,
one on the earth,
one between heaven and earth,
one on the people,
one on the birds,
one on the other animals,
one on the rivers,
one on the hills,
one on the fields with growing crops,
one on the lands with growing grass,
one on the riverbanks where cotton was planted,
and one on the mountains where buckwheat was planted.
They shone in all directions
and on everything in the world.

How did the cloud and the mist come into being?
How did the mountain wind form?
How did the thunder
and lightening come about in the sky?

① Momi: the god of heaven in Hani legends.

天上的俄求①想霸占地，
地上的卑甲阿玛②想霸占天，
两个互不相让，
拿起大刀争斗起来。
从地上打到天上，
从天上打到地上。

俄求呼出来的气成云雾，
卑甲阿玛呼出来的气成山风。
它们的吼声变成雷鸣，
它们的汗水变成雨点，
它们的刀碰撞在一处，
冒出的火星变成闪电。

最初人种是从哪里来？
长得像个什么样？
男的名字叫什么？
女的名字叫哪样？

最初的时候，
莫米从天上派下两个人种，
男的叫依沙然哈③，

① 俄求：据说是龙的变种。
② 卑甲阿玛：哈尼族传说中的一种动物。
③ 依沙然哈：哈尼族传说中的人种神。依沙，是名字；然哈，有“男人”之意。

Eqiu① in heaven wanted to own the earth,
while Beijiaama② on earth wanted to own the heaven,
Neither of them would give in,
so they took up the broadswords and fought,
fighting from earth to heaven,
and from heaven to earth.

The breath Eqiu exhaled turned into the cloud and mist,
while the breath Beijiaama exhaled turned into the mountain wind.
Their roar became the thunder,
and their sweat turned into raindrops.
When their broadswords clashed,
sparks came out and turned into the lightning.

Where did the first seeds of human come from?
What did they look like?
What was the man called?
and what was the woman called?

At the very beginning,
Momi sent two seeds of human from the heaven.
The man was called Yisha Ranha③,

---

① Eqiu: (It was) said to be a variant of dragon.

② Beijiaama: an animal in Hani legends.

③ Yisha Ranha: the god of human seeds in Hani legends. Yisha is the name; Ranha means "male".

女的叫依莫然玛①。
每人只有一只独眼，
长在脑门正中间。

依沙和依莫结成夫妻，
生下一个葫芦团。
过了七天七夜，
葫芦里响起声音。
刚把葫芦划开，
跳出很多人来，
仔细数数看看，
共有七十七种人……

七十七种人生成一副模样，
一个也不像依沙和依莫：
一只大大的独眼睛，
长在后脑壳上；
眼睛在一边，
脚手在一边，
要倒着走路，
做起活来像扯羊肚肠。

莫米看到这种人，
他的心一点也不来②；

① 依莫然玛：哈尼族传说中的人种神。依莫，是名字；然玛，有“女人”之意。

② 心不来：不喜欢。

and the woman was called Yimo Ranma①.
Each had only a single eye,
growing in the middle of the forehead.

Yisha and Yimo became husband and wife,
and they gave birth to a gourd.
After seven days and nights,
sounds came from inside of the gourd.
The moment the gourd was cut open,
many people jumped out,
A careful count showed,
there were seventy-seven of them…

Those seventy-seven looked like each other,
but none was like Yisha or Yimo:
Their big single eye,
grew on the back of their head.
The eye grew on one side,
while the hands and foot grew on the other.
They walked backwards,
and when they worked it was like pulling sheep's intestines.

When Momi saw this kind of humans,
he was not happy②,

① Yimo Ranma: the goddess of human seeds in Hani legends. Yimo is the name; Ranma means "female".

② He doesn't like them.

要换人种啰，
要生新的一代啰。

后脑独眼一代死了，
换了一代新人种。
这代新人种，
长着两只眼睛了。

可是这两只眼睛，
分别长在两个膝盖上。
新人种只顾脚不顾手，
做起活来东倒西歪。
莫米看到这种人，
他的心一点也不来；
要换人种啰，
要生新的一代啰。

莫米的心又不来，
人种换了一代又一代。
不知过了多少年，
又生出新的人一代。
这代人的眼睛有两只，
齐齐地长在鼻子边上；
和现在的人一个样，
做起活来也方便。

莫米看到这代人，

so he wanted to change to another kind of humans,
and to give birth to a new generation.

After those with the only eye on the back of their head died,
a new kind of humans replaced them.
This generation of humans,
had two eyes.

But their two eyes
grew respectively on their two knees.
The new kind of humans only paid attention to their feet, but not their hands
so when they worked they swayed left and right.
When Momi saw this kind of humans,
he wasn't happy.
He wanted to replace them,
and to give birth to a new generation.

Momi was disappointed
from one generation to another generation.
No one knew how many years had passed,
before another new generation was born.
People of this generation had two eyes,
growing neatly on the two sides of their nose,
just like the people today,
so that they could work easily.

When Momi saw this generation,

心头老实喜欢。
从此不再换人种，
叫人代代照着这代人样生。

从此不知过了多少年，
不知过了多少代，
不论到天边，
不论到海边，
不论到哪里，
世间人都是一个样：
两只眼睛长在鼻子上边。

最初的兽种怎样来？
最初的鸟种怎样来？
撒兽种的是哪个？
撒鸟种的是哪个？
依沙然哈撒兽种，
依莫然玛撒鸟种。

依沙然哈把兽种撒在地上，
兽种很快变成螃蟹。
螃蟹进水抱蛋，
抱出七十七种走兽。

he really liked it.
He never changed the human kind again
and asked that they multiplied according to the same kind for future generations.

No one knew how many years had passed,
or how many generations had passed,
but whether it was the edges of heaven,
or the ends of the earth
or anywhere in between,
humans in the world were the same:
their two eyes grew above their noses.

How did the first seeds of the other animals come about?
and the first seeds of the birds?
Who sowed the seeds of the other animals?
and the seeds of the birds?
It was Yisha Ranha who sowed the seeds of the other animals
and Yimo Ranma who sowed the seeds of the birds.

When Yisha Ranha sowed the seeds of other animals on the ground,
they soon became crabs.
They went into the water to hatch eggs,
and produced seventy-seven kinds of four-foot animals.

依莫然玛把鸟种撒到天上，
鸟种很快变成蝙蝠。
大风把蝙蝠吹碎，
变成七十七种飞鸟。

最初草种怎样来？
最初树种怎样来？
撒草种的是哪个？
撒树种的是哪个？
依沙然哈撒下草种，
依莫然玛撒下树种。

草种很快长成谷子，
一粒谷子像拳头一样大。
马蹄踏碎谷子，
变成七十七种粮食。

树种很快长成大树，
一个果子像磨盘一样大。
鸟雀啄破果子，
变成七十七种树木。

哈木①把地界划出来，
戛卡②把大路辟出来，
欧卡③把水沟开出来，

---

① 哈木：哈尼语，即鹌鹑。

②③ 戛卡、欧卡：均为哈尼语，两种动物的名称。下文的“喝泽美膀”意同。

When Yimo Ranma scattered the seeds of the birds into the sky,
they soon became bats.
The strong wind blew the bats into pieces,
which turned into seventy-seven kinds of birds.

How did the first seeds of the grass come about?
and the first seeds of the tree ?
Who sowed the seeds of the grass?
and the seeds the trees?
Yisha Ranha sowed the seeds of the grass
and Yimo Ranma, the seeds of the trees.

The grass seeds soon grew into the crops,
and each grain was as big as a fist.
After the horses trampled them,
they turned into seventy-seven kinds of cereals.

The seeds of the tree soon grew into big trees,
and each fruit was as big as a millstone.
After birds pecked broken the fruits,
the fruits became seventy-seven kinds of fruit trees.

Hamu① marked out the various areas,
Gaka② opened up the roads,
Ouka③ made the ditches,

① Hamu: quail in the Hani language.

②③ Gaka, Oka: names of two kinds of animals in the Hani language, the following Heze Meibang is also the name of an animal.

螃蟹把水分出来，
鸭子把水引出来，
喝泽美膀把田造出来。

阿妣仰遮①把寨子建起来，
欧巴、欧牛②把寨名取出来，
遮依、遮车③把水井挖出来，
欧比吉莫、龙冲牛斗④把水井管起来，
可阿、可遮⑤把房子盖起来，
收洛阿秋⑥把火种燃起来。

天有了，
地有了，
天上样样都有了，
一样东西也不差；
地上万物都有了，
一样东西也不少。
天神住在天上高兴了，
地神住在地上喜欢了。

众人：萨——萨⑦！

---

① 阿妣仰遮：哈尼族传说中的建寨女始祖。
② 欧巴、欧牛：哈尼族传说中的取寨名的始祖。
③ 遮依、遮车：哈尼族传说中的建水井的始祖。
④ 欧比吉莫、龙冲牛斗：哈尼族传说中的管水的始祖。
⑤ 可阿、可遮：哈尼族传说中的盖房的始祖。
⑥ 收洛阿秋：哈尼族传说中的播火种的始祖。
⑦ 哈尼族歌手演唱完一节或一段诗歌后，听众的附和声。

crabs separated the water out,
ducks led it to
the fields Heze Meibang created.

Api Yangzhe① built the villages,
Ouba, Ouniu② named them,
Zheyi and Zheche③ dug the wells,
Oubi Jimo and Longchong Niudou④ managed the wells,
Ke'a and Kezhe⑤ built the houses,
and Shouluo Aqiu⑥ lit the fire.

Now there was the heaven,
and the earth,
things of all kinds in the heaven,
with nothing in shortage,
and things of all kinds on the earth,
with nothing lacking.
The god of heaven was happy to live in heaven,
and the god of earth was happy to live on earth.

Everyone: Sa—Sa⑦!

---

① Api Yangzhe: female village-making ancestor in Hani legends.

② Ouba, Ouniu: ancestors who named villages in Hani legends.

③ Zheyi and Zheche: well-digging ancestors in Hani legends

④ Oubi Jimo and Longchong Niudou: well-managing ancestors in Hani legends.

⑤ Ke'a and Kezhe: house-building ancestors in Hani legends.

⑥ Shouluo Aqiu: tinder spreading ancestor in Hani legends.

⑦ The audience's cheer after the Hani singer finishes a section of the song.

二、牡普谜帕[①]

萨啦阿依——
天风从天上吹下来，
地风从地下冒出来；
天风呼啦啦离地三脚掌，
地风呼啦啦离天三巴掌。
天风和地风碰在一起，
天地摇晃着轰隆作响。

天地之间没有柱子支撑，
天塌下来了，
地翻上来了；
洪水淹没大地，
洪水淹到天上，
分不清天边地边在哪里。

① 牡普谜帕：哈尼语，有天翻地覆的意思。

Ⅱ. Mupumipa[1]

Sala'ayi—

The heavenly wind blew down from the sky,

and the earthly wind blew up from the ground.

The heavenly wind was howling three feet above the ground,

while the earthly wind was howling three palms away from the sky.

When the heavenly wind and the earthly wind collided,

heaven and earth rocked and roared.

With no supporting pillars between heaven and earth,

the heaven fell down,

and the earth surged up;

The earth was flooded,

and the heaven was inundated,

so heaven and earth became indistinguishable again.

① Mupumipa: It has the connotation that the world is turned upside down in the Hani language.

大人淹死完了，
小娃淹死完了；
男人淹死完了，
女人淹死完了。
世上只剩下莫鲁和沙崩两兄妹，
躲在一个大葫芦里漂在洪水上。

不知过了多少年月，
洪水渐渐退下去。
大水退到哪里，
葫芦也漂到哪里。
大水退到汪洋大海，
葫芦却挂在一棵大松树上。

兄妹俩钻出葫芦一看，
上不沾天下不着地，
头上是云雾翻滚，
脚下是万丈深渊。
哥哥愁得皱眉头，
妹妹急得淌眼泪。

高高的松树上，
老鹰筑有窝；
窝里三只小鹰叫，
探头张嘴等待老鹰来喂食。

The adults drowned,
so did the children,
the men,
and the women.
The world had but two siblings left, Molu and Shabeng,
who hid in a big gourd floating on the floodwater.

No one knew how many years had passed,
before the floodwater receded.
Wherever the floodwater went,
wherever the gourd was.
But when the floodwater retreated into the sea,
the gourd was hanging on a big pine tree.

The two siblings got out of the gourd and saw,
they could neither touch the sky nor reach the ground.
Above their heads were rolling clouds,
and below their feet was an abyss of 100, 000 feet.
The older brother frowned out of anxiety,
while the younger sister wept out of worry.

On the tall pine tree,
some eagles had built a nest,
where three baby eagles were crying,
craning their necks, opening their mouths, and waiting for the mother eagle to feed them.

一条毒蛇爬上树，
吐着分叉的长舌头，
倏倏扑向老鹰窝。
小鹰要飞飞不起，
小鹰要跳跳不动；
三只小鹰被吓坏，
可可怜怜挤作一团，
吱吱地哭叫喊爹妈。

兄妹俩看见心着急，
想好主意爬到树梢，
各人劈下一根松枝，
奋力把毒蛇打死。
他们将毒蛇掐断，
一截一截给鹰儿喂食。

老鹰寻食回来了；
三只小鹰忙告诉爹妈：
“我们已经吃了一顿最好的饭菜，
肚子饱鼓鼓，
什么也吃不得了。”

老鹰听了感到奇怪，
就细细盘问小鹰：
“是谁好心喂你们，
孩儿都吃了些什么饭菜？”

A poisonous snake climbed up the tree,
flicking its long forked tongue,
it charged at the eagles' nest.
The three baby eagles tried to fly away but in vain,
and tried to jump up but failed.
Frightened,
they huddled together helplessly,
crying for their parents.

The two siblings witnessed this with great concern,
so they decided to climb up to the treetop,
They each snapped off a pine branch
and hit the snake hard till it died.
Then they cut the snake into pieces
and fed the baby eagles by the pieces.

When the parent eagles came back from hunting for food,
the three baby eagles told them :
"We have already had the best meal,
and our stomachs were too full
to eat anything else. "

The parent eagles were puzzled to hear this,
and asked the baby eagles for details:
"Who is so kind to feed you all?
What kind of food did you have?"

三只小鹰像芋头冒芽，
争着告诉爹妈：
“爹妈出窝去寻食，
有条毒蛇来吃我们；
这对兄妹来救命，
打死毒蛇喂饱我们蛇肉。”

老鹰听了心里感激，
扇着翅膀感谢兄妹俩：
“你们是心肠最好的人，
怪不得世间只剩你们；
你们搭救了我的孩子，
我们想法送你们到地上。”

兄妹俩担心老鹰背不动，
互相望望不出气。
老鹰猜透他们的心理，
张开翅膀飞到了地上，
一只翅膀背上一扇磨，
稳稳当当地回到松树上；
然后又把两扇磨，
轻轻送到地上。

兄妹俩见了好欢喜，
一股暖流涌上心房，
他们对老鹰点头，
他们向老鹰招手。

The three baby eagles were like the sprouting taros,
trying to be the one to tell their parents:
"When you left the nest to look for food,
a poisonous snake came to eat us.
It was the two siblings who came to our rescue,
killed the snake and fed us full with the snake meat."

On hearing this, the parent eagles were grateful and
flapped their wings to thank the two siblings:
"You are the kindest people.
No wonder you are the only ones left in the world.
Since you saved our children,
we would like to try and send you to the ground."

The two siblings were worried that they were too heavy for the eagles to carry,
so they just looked at each other silently.
The parent eagles guessed what was on their minds,
and they spread their wings and flew to the ground.
They carried a millstone on each of their wings
and flew back steadily to the pine trees.
Then they carried the two millstones again
and returned them gently to the ground.

The two siblings were joyful to see this
and felt warmth at the bottom of their heart.
They nodded to the parent eagles
and waved to them.

公老鹰张开翅膀，
把哥哥莫鲁背下地；
母老鹰张开翅膀，
把妹妹沙崩背到地上。

兄妹俩到了地上，
哥哥对妹妹讲：
“你到东边找一找，
看看还有没有挖田的男人；
我到西边看一看，
瞧瞧还有没有砍柴的姑娘。”

哥哥往西边去了，
妹妹朝东边走了，
九座山跑遍不见一个脚印，
九条冲走遍听不到一样声音。
他们找遍东南西北，
四面八方没有一个人影。
不知找了多少天，
每天只是两兄妹遇在一起。

世上没有其他女人哟，
哥哥莫鲁找不着妻子；
世上没有其他男人哟，
妹妹沙崩找不着丈夫。
眼看世间快要绝人种，
想到宽宽大地缺主人，

The father eagle spread his wings,
bringing Molu down to the ground,
and the mother eagle spread her wings,
carrying Shabeng back to the ground.

After the two siblings were on the ground,
the older brother said to his younger sister:
"Go to the east,
to see if there are still men digging the fields.
I will go to the west,
to see if there are still women cutting the firewood."

The older brother went to the west,
and the younger sister went to the east.
They ran through nine mountains but didn't find a single footprint,
walked by nine streams but didn't hear a sound.
They searched everywhere,
but there was no one anywhere.
No one knew how many days had passed,
but everyday only the two siblings came back to each other.

There were no other women in the world,
so the older brother Molu couldn't find a wife;
There were no other men in the world,
so the younger sister Shabeng couldn't find a husband.
Seeing that the humankind was about to become extinct,
seeing that owners were needed in the vast land,

哥哥急得像老水牛喘粗气，
妹妹失望得淌眼泪。

一个天气晴朗的日子，
兄妹俩来到一条河边。
哥哥对妹妹说：
“活着的人一处也找不着，
我们两兄妹难生活了；
用树叶测测看吧，
也许它们能告诉我们怎么办。”

哥哥先摘一片水冬瓜叶子，
轻轻丢进河水里；
妹妹也摘一片水冬瓜叶子，
跟着哥哥丢进河水里。

两片叶子翻上翻下漂，
顺着河水淌下去。
哥哥追着树叶跑，
妹妹追着树叶跑。

叶子淌到河尾沙滩上，
两片叶子合拢在一起：
哥哥的叶子在上面，
妹妹的叶子在下面。

一个天气暖和的日子，
兄妹俩来到一座高山上。

Molu was so anxious he breathed heavily like an old buffalo,
and Shabeng wept tears of frustration.

On a sunny day,
the brother and sister came by a river.
The older brother said to the younger sister:
"We cannot find a living soul anywhere,
and could hardly live on like this.
let's use leaves to do a test,
for maybe they can tell us what to do."

The older brother picked a leaf from an alnus first,
and gently threw it into the river;
The sister picked another alnus leaf,
and threw it into the river, too.

The two leaves were tumbling with the waves,
flowing down along the river.
The older brother ran after the leaves,
so did the younger sister.

When the leaves flowed to the beach at the end of the river,
they came together:
The older brother's leave was on top,
and the sister's was at the bottom.

On a warm day,
the brother and the sister came to a high mountain.

妹妹对哥哥说：
“世上没有其他活着的人了，
我们不会生活下去。
滚石头测测看吧，
也许石头会告诉我们怎么办。”

妹妹拣了一块石头，
哥哥拣了一块石头；
妹妹先把石头滚下山，
哥哥也跟着把石头滚下山。

两块石头翻着跟斗滚下去，
兄妹俩跟着跑下山去看。
石头滚到山脚，
两块石头合拢叠在一起：
哥哥的石头在上面，
妹妹的石头在下面。

妹妹看见石头，
羞红的脸像一朵花，
转过背去不说话。

哥哥看见石头，
红着脸对妹妹说：
“亲亲的阿妹哟，
树叶子测过了，

The younger sister said to her older brother:
"There are no other living people in the world,
and we can't live like this.
Let's use the rock stones to do a test,
for maybe the stones will tell us what to do."

The sister picked up a rock,
and the brother picked up one too.
The younger sister rolled the rock down the mountainside first,
and then the older brother rolled the rock down the mountainside.

While the rocks somersaulted down the mountainside,
the brother and the sister followed behind them running.
When the rocks reached the foot of the mountain,
they landed on top of each other:
the older brother's rock was on top,
while the younger sister's rock was at the bottom.

When the sister saw the rocks,
she blushed like a flower,
turned her back, said not a word.

When the brother saw the rocks,
he said to his sister, blushing:
"My dear sister,
we have tried the tree-leaves,

石头也测过了。
放河水漂的树叶，
最后是叠在一起；
从山上滚下去的石头，
最后是摞在一起。
不想见也见着了，
想见也见着了，
世上活着的只有我们兄妹，
我们到底该怎么办？”

妹妹低着头，
像蚊子哼一样细声：
“问问莫托库鲁舍①
他咋个说就咋个办。”

兄妹俩对着苍天叩头，
齐声向苍天呼喊：
“仁慈的莫托库鲁舍啊，
洪水滔天人间受灾难，
世上的人都死完了，
只剩下我们兄妹了。
求你不要让世间绝人种，
给我们指永生的路吧！”

① 莫托库鲁舍：哈尼族传说中的天神之一。

and the rocks.
The leaves floating in the water
overlapped in the end;
the rocks rolling down the mountainside
laid on top of each other in the end.
We both saw what we didn't want to see,
as well as what we wanted to see.
Only we two are alive in the world,
so what should we do?"

The sister lowered her head,
whispering like a mosquito:
"Ask Motuokulushe①
and we will do what he says."

The brother and sister kowtowed to the heaven,
pleading aloud together:
"Oh, merciful Motuokulushe,
people in the world suffered terribly from the big flood,
and all people died,
except for us two siblings.
Please don't let the humankind die out,
by pointing the humankind to eternal life!"

① MotuoKulushe: one of the gods of heaven in Hani legends.

天空忽然闪现一道金光，
同时传来一个声音：
“世间数你们兄妹俩心最好，
我特意把你们留下。
你们兄妹成一家，
你们兄妹做夫妻，
男耕女织传人种，
一代一代人会兴旺。”

哥哥听了对妹妹说：
“亲亲的阿妹哟，
莫托库鲁舍的话你听见了，
为了传人种，
我们就做夫妻吧。”

妹妹用手蒙着脸说：
“亲亲的阿哥，
害羞也顾不得了，
就听莫托库鲁舍的话，
我们就成一家吧。”

兄妹俩成了一家，
兄妹俩做了夫妻，
为了传人种，
辛辛苦苦生儿育女。

Suddenly a golden light flashed in the sky,
accompanied with a voice:
"You two siblings are the most kind-hearted people in the world,
so I kept you two alive in this world on purpose.
You two siblings will make a family,
and become husband and wife.
the man will plough and the woman weave,
to reproduce and thrive generation after generation."

Hearing that, the older brother said to the younger sister:
"My dear sister,
You have heard what Motuokulushe said.
In order to continue the humankind,
let's be husband and wife."

The younger sister covered her face with her hands and replied:
"My dear brother,
this is no time to dwell on our own shyness.
Let's follow what Motuokulushe said,
and form a family."

The older brother and his younger sister got married,
and became husband and wife.
In order to continue the humankind,
they worked hard to bear children.

他们生了三个儿子,
他们生了三个姑娘。

儿子姑娘一天天长大了,
莫鲁和沙崩心里像装了一缸蜜糖。
一把荞子绿一片,
一股龙潭水润一方,
为了快快繁衍人类,
他们把儿女打发到四面八方。

听说要到别的地方,
大儿子心里老实欢喜:
“亲亲的阿爸阿妈,
我人大脚杆粗,
让我到高山上去吧,
两个弟弟留在平坝。”

听说大哥要到高山去,
二儿子也说出了自己的想法:
“亲亲的阿爸阿妈,
我的体力好,
让我到半山去吧,
留下弟弟在平坝。”

三儿子听了哥哥们的话,
心里有些气不平:
“阿爸和阿妈,

They gave birth to three boys,
and three girls.

Their sons and daughters grew up day by day.

Molu and Shabeng felt their hearts were filled up with a jar of honey.

A handful of buckwheat seeds greened a field,
and a stream of Longtan water moistened the land.
To let the humankind grow quickly,
they sent their children in all directions.

Hearing that they would go somewhere else,
the first son was really happy:
"Dear papa and mama,
I am big and strong.
Let me go to the high mountains
and leave the two younger brothers down here."

Hearing the first brother was going to the mountains.
their second son also expressed his thoughts:
"Dear papa and mama,
I am in great shape.
Let me go half way up the mountains,
and leave the youngest brother down here."

The third son heard what his brothers said,
felt a little unfair in his heart:
"Dear papa and mama,

我人小会长大，
让我和哥哥们在一起，
相亲相爱不分离。”

莫鲁和沙崩开导儿子：
“我的儿哟，
传人种是天神的意思，
你们不能为了弟兄的情意，
耽误了人间的大事。
你们同是一个父母养，
大家同是一个父母生，
手心手背都是肉，
树枝树叶连着根；
不管到天头地脚，
永远是亲亲的一家弟兄。”

一家人商量好了，
弟兄们要分开了。
莫鲁和沙崩心里高兴，
把道理讲给儿女们听：
“大水淹没人世的时候，
多亏纳米堵合①的青松将我们搭救，
孩儿不管到了什么地方，
遇到松树要磕头拜礼。

① 纳米堵合：哈尼语，即一座高山。

young as I am, I will grow up someday.
Let me be with my brothers,
we will love each other and never separate."

Molu and Shabeng said to their sons:
"My dear sons,
to reproduce is the will of the god of heaven,
so brotherhood is secondary
to your responsibility to the world.
You were raised by the same parents,
and were born to the same parents,
we love you all the same,
like roots that are connected to the branches and leaves;
wherever you go, the top of the heaven or the bottom of the earth,
you will always be brothers of one family."

They came up with a plan,
and the brothers were about to go their separate ways.
Molu and Shabeng were happy,
asked their children of one thing:
"When the world was flooded,
it was a pine tree on the Namiduhe ① that saved us.
My children, no matter where you go,
kowtow and salute to pine trees whenever you see them.

① Namiduhe: a mountain in the Hani language.

"每年过节的日子，
要把青松接来家里，
要给它烧香磕头，
还要用酒肉饭菜献祭。"

大儿子大姑娘配一对，
到高山安家去了；
二儿子二姑娘配一对，
到半山腰安家去了；
三儿子三姑娘配一对，
到平地安家去了。

火苗亮闪闪，
烟火冲上天，
人间又有人种了，
莫托库鲁舍看见心欢喜。

为了让人种一代一代传下去，
为了让人类一代一代快发展，
不能让天再塌下来，
不能让地再翻过来；
要把天锁起来，
要把地锁起来。

莫托库鲁舍想出办法，
派来阿朗、阿汪①两位神主，

① 阿朗、阿汪：哈尼族传说中两位锁天锁地的神。

"For every festival of the year,
get the pine tree home.
Burn incense for it, kowtow to it,
and offer sacrifice of wine and meat to it."

The first son and the first daughter became a couple
and settled down on the top of the mountains;
The second son and the second daughter became a couple
and settled down halfway up the mountains;
and the third son and the third daughter became a couple,
and settled down on the plains.

The flames were shining,
with the smokes rushing to the sky,
The world had the humankind again,
the sight of which pleased Motuokulushe very much.

To ensure that the humankind could continue generation after generation,
and develop from generation to generation,
they could not let the heaven fall again,
or the earth surge up again.
Heaven must be locked in place,
and so must be the earth.

Motuokulushe came up with an idea:
he sent two gods: Alang and Awang①

① Alang, Awang: the gods for securing heaven and earth in Hani legends.

在天和地中间立柱子，
把天撑起来，
把地压下来，
用锁把天锁起来，
用锁把地锁起来。

阿朗拿来天神的柱子，
选好立柱子的地基：
东边立起金柱子，
南边立起银柱子，
西边立起铜柱子，
北边立起铁柱子。

阿汪拿来天神的大锁，
把天地的四方锁起来：
东方用金锁锁起来，
南方用银锁锁起来，
西方用铜锁锁起来，
北方用铁锁锁起来。

阿朗立好柱子，
向万物发了誓言，
打下木刻作记号：
大公鸡的冠子上打了刻，
老水牛的角上打了刻，
山羊的角上打了刻，
蛇的身上打了刻，
哈尼妇女的包头上打了刻，
从此天不会塌下来。

to set up pillars between heaven and earth
that held up the heaven,
and push down the earth.
They then locked in place both the heaven
and the earth.

Alang used the pillars from the gods of the heaven
and selected the foundations for them:
a gold pillar in the east,
a silver pillar in the south,
a copper pillar in the west,
and an iron one in the north.

Awang used the big locks from the gods of heaven,
to lock in place the four sides of both the heaven and the earth:
a gold lock for the east,
a silver lock for the south,
a copper lock for the west,
and an iron one for the north.

After Alang finished setting up the pillars,
he vowed to all things,
and marked them with woodcuts:
on the crowns of the big cocks,
on the horns of the old buffaloes,
on the horns of the goats,
on the bodies of the snakes,
and on the Hani women's turbans.
From then on, the heaven would not fall down.

阿汪锁好锁，
向万物发了誓言，
打下木刻作记号：
老虎的身上打了刻，
豹子的身上打了刻，
彝家女人的衣边上打了刻，
傣家姑娘的裙子上打了刻，
汉人妇女的小脚上打了刻，
从此地不会翻过来。

天地中间立起了柱子，
天地锁上了神锁，
阿朗、阿汪发了誓言，
阿朗、阿汪打下了刻，
天不会塌下来了，
地不会翻过来了。
人种一代一代传下来了，
人类一代一代发起来了。

众人：萨——萨！

After Awang locked in place all sides of heaven and earth,
he vowed to all things,
and marked them with woodcuts:
on the bodies of the tigers,
on the bodies of leopards,
on the edges of the Yi women's clothing
on the Dai girls' skirts,
and on the Han women's tiny feet.
From then on, the earth would stay down.

After pillars were set up between heaven and earth,
with heaven and earth locked in place,
Alang and Awang made vows,
and made marks.
The heaven wouldn't fall down,
and the earth wouldn't surge up.
The humankind has continued from generation to generation,
and developed generation after generation.

Everyone: Sa—Sa!

三、昂煞息思①

萨啦阿依——
自从天翻地覆，
洪水淹没大地，
树木和草淹死了，
留着的树木草种冲走了，
藏着的五谷种子冲走了，
大地一片光秃秃，
草木五谷一样也不长。
世上的人们不会过日子，
祈求莫米给种子。

仁慈的莫米告诉人们：
“树种没被水冲走，
草种没被水冲走，
五谷种子没被水冲走，
都被大鱼吃进肚子里。

① 昂煞息思：哈尼语，即杀鱼取种。

Ⅲ. Angshaxisi[①]

Sala'ayi—
Ever since heaven and earth were turned upside down,
the earth was flooded,
trees and grass were killed,
the remaining tree- and grass-seeds were washed away,
and the stored seeds of various cereals were swept away,
the earth was bare,
and none of the grass, trees, and crops would revive.
People in the world didn't know how to live their lives,
so they prayed to Momi to give them some seeds.

The kind Momi told them:
"The tree seeds were not washed away,
nor were the grass seeds,
or the cereal seeds.
They are all in the stomach of a big fish who ate them.

① Angshaxisi: killing the fish to get the roe in the Hani language.

"赶快找葛麻，
织张大渔网，
大江大河浪滔滔，
大鱼就在水里藏，
快把大鱼打上来，
杀死大鱼取回种。"

不知葛根长在哪里？
不知葛根窜在什么地方？
比出阿玛玛学①去问野猪，
好心肠的野猪说：
"葛根深深埋地下，
葛根窜到大河边。"

九个姑娘去寻葛根藤，
倒钩刺把衣裳撕成碎片。
走了三天路，
翻过九座山，
大河边上绿汪汪，
到处是老水牛拉不断的葛藤。

九个姑娘九把刀哟，
大河边上采葛藤，
采一根只有一把，

① 比出阿玛玛学：哈尼族传说中最先打鱼的人。

"Hurry to find some kudzu vines,
and use it to weave a big fishing net,
for in the surging river waves,
the big fish is hiding,
Hurry and catch the big fish
so as to kill it and get back the seeds."

Where did the kudzu vine grow?
How far did it spread?
Bichu'amamaxue① went to ask the boar.
The kind-hearted boar said:
"Kudzu is buried deep under the ground,
and it spreads to the big riverside."

Nine young women went to look for the kudzu vine,
their clothes torn into pieces by barb thorns.
After they had walked for three days,
and climbed over nine mountains,
they came to the green-covered banks of a big river,
with the kudzu vine so strong that old water buffaloes could not break.

Nine women with their nine knives,
reaped the kudzu vines by the river.
They could pick one at a time,

---

① Bichu'amamaxue: the first person who captured the fish according to Hani legends.

割一千根才满一背；
不怕采葛活计苦，
不怕背葛藤腰杆酸疼，
一根一把割出来，
一背一背背回来。

剥下葛藤皮，
撕出麻丝纺细线；
纺一根只有一绕，
纺完一千根才有一捆。

姑娘剥葛皮从早到晚，
纺葛麻从黑夜到天亮。
一根一根葛藤剥下皮，
一捆一捆葛麻纺成线。

用线来织网，
织几下才是一个眼；
织千眼万眼，
才能织成一张渔网。
手指头划破出血不怕，
手掌心磨出老茧不怕，
一眼一眼地织，
千眼万眼织出了渔网。

十个伙子抬渔网，
大河里头撒大鱼。
织成的渔网撒不开，

and they had to pick a thousand to fill their back-basket.
They didn't mind the hard work,
or the backaches,
one vine at a time,
one back-basket at a time.

They peeled off the vine skins,
and then split out the hemp silk thread for spinning the yarn.
A vine made only one loop,
and it took a thousand to make a skein.

They peeled the kudzu vine from morning to night,
and spun hemp threads from dark to dawn.
They peeled off the vine one by one,
and spun the threads skein by skein.

Weaving a net by threads,
they stitched a few times to make a hole,
and it took tens of thousands of holes
to weave a fishing net.
They didn't care that their fingertips were cut bleeding
and their palms grew callouses.
One hole at a time,
they made a net with tens of thousands of holes.

Ten men carried the net,
and they cast it into the big river to catch the big fish,
but the woven fishing net wouldn't spread,

漂在水上乱成一团；
原来网脚要有铅巴坠，
渔网才会撒开沉入水。

渔网需要铅巴坠，
哪里有铅巴？
一个认不得，
一个也没有，
要到各个地方赶街子，
去寻找铅巴坠渔网。

先去赶羊街，
羊街街子好热闹，
赶街人像地里的甘蔗一样密，
喧哗声像打闷雷一样响。

赶街的人样样都有：
穿宽袖衣的傣家女人来了，
戴公鸡帽的彝家姑娘来了，
背秤杆的汉人小伙子来了，
会打麂子的瑶家汉子来了；
各种各样的人都来了，
四面八方的人都来了。

转来转去地找，
转到街头找。
街头用的东西样样都有卖，
唯独铅巴没人卖。

floating on the water in a mess.
It turned out the net needed to be weighed down with lead at the corners,
so that the net could spread and sink into the water.

The fishing net needed lead net-weights,
but where was lead?
No one could recognize it,
and no one had one.
They had to go to the street fairs in various places
to look for lead to make the fishing-net-weights.

They first went to the Yangjie street fair,
where it was quite lively.
People in the street market were as many as sugarcanes in the fields,
they sounded like muffled thunder.

People who went to the fair were of all kinds:
Dai women in wide-sleeved tunics,
Yi young women wearing cockscomb-shaped hats,
Han business men with scales on their backs,
Yao hunters of muntjacs.
They were people of all kinds,
and from everywhere.

The Hani walked around,
and came to the entrance of the street.
They found everything usable there
except for lead.

转来转去找，
转到街中找。
街中穿的东西样样都有卖，
唯独铅巴没人卖。

转来转去找，
转到街尾找。
街尾吃的东西样样都有卖，
唯独铅巴没人卖。

买不到铅巴不能回家，
还要到别处街子去找。
赶了羊街赶猪街，
赶了猪街赶牛街，
转到郎特①赶龙街，
转到阿丕②赶马街，
倮玛③鼠街赶过了，
仰书垤④街赶过了，
托普⑤街子赶过了，
青尼⑥街子赶过了。
街上样样东西都有卖，
唯独铅巴没人卖。

---

① 郎特：地名。
② 阿丕：地名。
③ 倮玛：地名。
④ 仰书垤：地名。
⑤ 托普：地名。
⑥ 青尼：地名。

They walked around again
and came to the middle of the street.
They found everything wearable there
except for lead.

They walked around again
and came to the end of the street.
They found everything edible there
except for lead.

They would not go home without the lead,
so they went to look for it in other fairs,
From the Yangjie fair to the Zhujie one
from the Zhujie fair to the Niujie one,
then to the Longjie fair in Langte①.
They went to the Majie fair in Api②
the Shujie fair in Luoma③,
the fair in Yangshuzhi④,
the fair in Tuopu⑤,
the fair in Qingni⑥.
They found things of every kinds
except for lead.

---

① Langte: name of a place.
② Api: name of a place.
③ Luoma: name of a place.
④ Yangshuzhi: name of a place.
⑤ Tuopu: name of a place.
⑥ Qingni: name of a place.

转来转去看，
遇着慈戛戈欧①姑娘欧巴、欧牛，
问她们见不见有铅巴卖。
两个姑娘回答说：
“铅巴这里有，
用铅巴一样重的银子来换。”

没有铅巴打不着大鱼，
拿出银子买回铅巴。
银亮亮的铅巴刺眼睛，
男人女人见了心里老实喜欢，
请来傣家师傅打网坠，
铅巴网脚沉甸甸。

选了最好的日子，
择了最好的时辰，
抬着大渔网，
大河里头打大鱼。

头回撒下去，
不见渔网动，
只见水泡泡，
没有撒到鱼。

① 慈戛戈欧：地名。

They looked and looked,
and then they met two young women Ouba and Ouniu from Cigage'ou①,
When they asked if there was lead for sale,
the two young women replied:
"We have lead.
You can use silver of the same weight to trade for it."

Without lead, they couldn't catch the big fish,
so they paid silver for the lead.
The shiny lead dazzled the eyes,
and the men and women were very happy to see it.
They invited a Dai blacksmith to make the lead weights,
which now weighed heavily on the corners of the fishing net.

They chose an auspicious day
and the best hour,
to bring the big fishing net to the big river,
to catch the big fish.

After casting the fishing net for the first time,
they didn't see the net move,
except some bubbles.
They did not catch the fish.

① Cigage'ou: name of a place.

二回撒下去，
不见渔网动，
只见泥渣和树叶，
还是没有撒到鱼。

三回撒下去，
渔网不停地动，
渔网不停地晃。
十个伙子拉起网，
撒着一条大鱼了，
放在河边沙滩上。

鱼头黄得闪金光，
鱼尾花得刺眼睛，
鱼眼睁得碗样大，
鱼在沙滩上乱蹦乱跳。

打着大鱼了，
寨头的阿波①来看，
寨尾的阿妣②来看，
男女老少都来看，
谁也说不出是什么鱼。

抬着两长的大鱼，
四处去问鱼名称。

① 阿波：阿爷。
② 阿妣：阿奶。

After casting the fishing net for the second time,
they didn't see the net move,
except mud and leaves.
They still did not catch the fish.

After casting the fishing net for the third time,
they saw the net kept moving,
the net kept swinging.
Ten guys pulled up the net,
where there was a big fish,
which they placed on the beach.

The head of the fish was so yellow it shined like gold.
The colorful tail of the fish was so bright it dazzled the eyes.
The eyes of the fish were as big as bowls,
and it was jumping about on the beach.

The big fish was caught,
Abo① living at the entrance of the village came to see it,
and so did Abi② living at the end of the village.
Men and women, young and old, all came to see it,
but no one could tell what kind of fish it was.

They carried this big fish with long head and long tail
around and asked others what fish it was.

---

① Abo: grandpa.
② Abi: grandma.

抬给罗比①看，抬给罗梅②看，
抬给布洪③看，
抬给阿松④看……
个个都摇头，
谁也说不出是什么鱼。

抬着两长的大鱼，
又到四方问鱼名。
汉人看过了，
傣家看过了，
彝家看过了，
瑶家看过了……
个个都摇头，
一个也认不出是哪样鱼。

不知是条哪样鱼，
人们心里老实着急。
对着苍天求莫米，
教教是条哪样鱼？

仁慈的莫米听见了，
传下话来给贝玛：

① 罗比：哈尼族的支系。
② 罗梅：哈尼族的支系。
③ 布洪：哈尼族的支系。
④ 阿松：哈尼族的支系。

They carried it to Luobi①,
to Luomei②,
to Buhong③,
to Asong④...
but they all shook their heads,
could not tell what fish it was.

They carried this big fish with long head and long tail,
and went again everywhere to ask others what fish it was.
The Han people saw it,
and then the Dai people,
the Yi people,
the Yao people...
but they all shook their heads,
could not recognize what fish it was.

Not knowing what kind of fish it was,
the Hani were very worried,
so they pleaded to Momi in heaven
to tell them what fish it was.

The merciful Momi heard their plea
and passed on a message to Beima:

---

① Luobi: a branch of the Hani people.
② Luomei: a branch of the Hani people.
③ Buhong: a branch of the Hani people.
④ Asong: a branch of the Hani people.

"那条大鱼肚里藏珍宝，
鱼名只有两个人知道：
一个是阿福根勒阿搓①，
一个是阿车克什也莫阿玛②。"

人们请来这两个能人，
才知道这条大鱼叫黄花鱼，
鱼肚里藏着草木和五谷种子，
等它闭上眼睛才能拿到。

要杀大鱼取种子，
先是抬到大江边去杀，
杀了鱼不死，
眼睛也不闭。
鱼为什么不会死？
鱼为什么不闭眼？
因为那里有鲨鱼做伴。

又抬到森林里去杀，
杀了鱼不死，
眼睛也不闭。
鱼为什么不会死？
鱼为什么不闭眼？
因为那里是砍柴的地方。

---

① 阿福根勒阿搓：哈尼族传说中的善识者。
② 阿车克什也莫阿玛：哈尼族传说中的善识者。

"That big fish has treasures in its belly,
but its name only two people know:
one is Afugenle'acuo①,
and the other is Achekeshiyemo'ama②."

They invited these two wise persons
and learned that the big fish was called yellow croaker,
that they could get the seeds of grass, trees and cereals in its belly
only when the fish was dead and had closed its eyes.

To kill the big fish for seeds,
they first took it to the riverside and tried to kill it there,
but the wounds they inflicted could not kill it,
and its eyes would not close.
Why wouldn't the fish die?
Why didn't it close its eyes?
It was because sharks there were accompanying it.

They then took it to the forest and tried to kill it there,
but the wounds they inflicted could not kill it,
and its eyes would not close.
Why wouldn't the fish die?
Why didn't it close its eyes?
It was because it was the place to cut firewood.

---

① Afugenle'acuo: The wise person according to Hani legends.
② Achekeshiyemo'ama: The wise person according to Hani legends.

又抬到田边去杀，
杀了鱼不死，
眼睛也不闭。
鱼为什么不会死？
鱼为什么不闭眼？
因为那里是薅秧丢杂草的地方。

又抬到水井边去杀，
杀了鱼不死，
眼睛也不闭。
鱼为什么不会死？
鱼为什么不闭眼？
因为那里是背水的地方。

又抬到猪槽边去杀，
杀了鱼不死，
眼睛也不闭。
鱼为什么不会死？
鱼为什么不闭眼？
因为那里是喂猪食的地方。

又抬到灶门前去杀，
杀了鱼不死，
眼睛也不闭。
鱼为什么不会死？
鱼为什么不闭眼？
因为那里是女人煮饭的地方。

They then took the fish to the field and tried to kill it there,
but the wounds they inflicted could not kill it,
and its eyes would not close.
Why wouldn't the fish die?
Why didn't it close its eyes?
It was because that was where people threw away the weeds they pulled.

They then took the fish by a well and tried to kill it there,
but the wounds they inflicted could not kill it,
and its eyes would not close.
Why wouldn't the fish die?
Why didn't it close its eyes?
It was because it was the place to fetch water.

They then put it by the pig trough and tried to kill it there,
but the wounds they inflicted could not kill the fish,
and its eyes would not close.
Why wouldn't the fish die?
Why didn't it close its eyes?
It was because it was the place to feed pigs.

They then put the fish in front of the wood-fired stove and tried to kill it there,
but the wounds they inflicted could not kill it,
and its eyes would not close.
Why wouldn't the fish die?
Why didn't it close its eyes?
It was because that was the place for women to cook meals.

又抬到哈扎比堵收机阿勒①去杀，
鱼不摇头不摆尾，
红彤彤的血淌成河水。
大鱼杀死了，
眼睛闭上了。

这条大鱼肉厚有两拃②，
鱼肚有千层；
拿着快刀亮闪闪，
一层一层剖鱼肚。

剐开第一层鱼肚，
里面装着三粒谷子。
谷子栽在什么地方？
长杨柳树的龙潭旁。

剖开第二层鱼肚，
里面装着三粒荞子。
荞子栽在什么地方？
长水冬瓜树的山坡上。

剖开第三层鱼肚，
里面装着三粒高粱子。
高粱子栽在什么地方？
长芦苇的山坡上。

---

① 哈扎比堵收机阿勒：古地名，地址不详。
② 两拃：一尺。

They then took to Hazabidushouji'ale① and tried to kill it there,
and the fish stopped shaking its head or wagging its tail.
Its red blood flew like a river.
The big fish was killed,
and its eyes were closed.

The flesh of this big fish was one-foot thick,
and its maw had thousands of layers.
They held sharp and shiny knives,
and cut the maw open layer by layer.

Cutting open the first layer,
they found three grains of rice.
Where should rice be planted ?
They planted it by the Longtan pool with willow trees.

Cutting open the second layer,
they found three buckwheat seeds.
Where should buckwheat be planted?
They planted it on the hillside with alnus trees.

Cutting open the third layer,
they found three sorghum seeds.
Where should sorghum be planted?
They planted on the hillside with reeds.

① Hazabidushouji'ale: an ancient place, location today unknown.

剖开第四层鱼肚，
里面装着三粒棉花子。
棉花栽在什么地方？
长尖刀草的矮山上。

剖开第五层鱼肚，
里面装着三粒包谷子。
包谷栽在什么地方？
长锥栗树的山上。

剖开第六层鱼肚，
里面装着三粒黄豆子。
黄豆栽在什么地方？
长杨梅树的山上。

剖开第七层鱼肚，
里面装着三粒南瓜子。
南瓜栽在什么地方？
长黄泡刺的地上。

剖开第八层鱼肚，
里面装着三粒麻子。
麻栽在什么地方？
淌水的冲沟旁。

剖开第九层鱼肚，
里面装着各种树种。

Cutting open the fourth layer,
they found three cotton seeds.
Where should cotton be planted?
They planted it on the low ridges with the hedyotis diffusa.

Cutting open the fifth layer,
they found three corn kernels.
Where should corn be planted?
They planted it on the mountains with chestnut trees.

Cutting open the sixth layer,
they found three soya beans.
Where should soya beans be planted?
They planted it on the mountains with waxberry trees.

Cutting open the seventh layer,
They found three pumpkin seeds.
Where should pumpkin be planted?
They planted it on the ground with the thorny plants growing yellow berries.

Cutting open the eighth layer,
they found three hemp seeds.
Where should hemp be planted?
They planted it by the ditches with running water.

Cutting open the ninth layer,
they found various tree seeds.

树种撒在什么地方？
撒在所有的山上。

剖开第十层鱼肚，
里面装着各种草种。
草种撒在什么地方？
地上水里草会长。

五谷子种都有了，
各种树种都有了，
各种草种都有了，
一样种也不差了。

人们年年栽五谷，
年年把种收藏，
一年一年传下去，
一代一代不绝种。

人们把树种撒在所有的山上，
人们把草种撒在地上水里，
从此山山岭岭长了树，
地上水里到处长了草。
大地穿上绿衣裳，
莫米见了心里老实喜欢。
树木世世代代不绝种，
杂草祖祖辈辈不绝种。

众人：萨——萨！

Where should tree seeds be sowed?
They sowed them on all the mountains.

Cutting open the tenth layer,
they found various grass seeds.
Where should grass seeds be sowed?
They sowed them on the ground with water.

They had the seeds of various cereals,
seeds of various tree,
seeds of various grass,
and there was not one kind of seed missing.

People planted various cereals every year,
and every year they kept some seeds,
which they passed on year after year,
so the seeds continued generation after generation.

They scattered the tree seeds on all the mountains,
and grass seeds in the water and on the ground.
From then on there were trees everywhere on the mountains,
and grass everywhere in the water and on the ground.
The earth was clothed in green,
which made Momi very happy.
The trees would never die out,
nor would the weeds.

Everyone: Sa—Sa!

四、阿资资斗①

萨啦阿依——
远远的烘阿宗娘②地方，
住着一家十兄妹，
九个哥哥成了家，
小妹的名字叫尖收。

尖收勤劳性平和，
一天给九个哥哥背九次水，
一天给九个哥哥砍九次柴；
每次背的水一样清，
每次砍的柴一样多。

九个哥哥是勾心，
把小妹尖收当牛马：
米饭不给她吃，
新衣不给她穿，
狗咬不帮她吆。

① 阿资资斗：哈尼语，砍树计日。
② 烘阿，古地名；宗娘，旁边的意思。

Ⅳ. Azizidou[1]

Sala'ayi—
By the remote Hong'e[2]
lived one family with ten siblings.
Nine brothers were married and had their own family,
except the youngest sister Jianshou.

Jianshou was hard-working and temperate in disposition,
fetching water nine times a day for her nine older brothers,
cutting firewood nine times a day for them, too.
The water she fetched was always clear,
and the firewood she cut was always the same amount.

But her nine older brothers were heartless,
treating their little sister as a slave:
They gave no rice for her to eat,
no new clothes for her to wear,
and no help when dogs bit her.

① Azizidou: Hani language, counting days by tree branches (the origin of days, months and years).

② Hong'e: name of an ancient place.

尖收一日哭三回天不黑，
尖收一夜醒三次天不亮，
尖收再也熬不下去了，
只得拿起讨饭棍，
淌着眼泪离开家；
她从高山讨到江河汇集的海边，
她从海边讨到江河源头的高山。

有天尖收讨饭来到阿姆山，
面前有块望不到边的大田。
大田水口七宽，
尖收拄着讨饭棍过田埂。
跳过田水口，
拄棍生了根，
忽然变成一棵大青树。

大青树遮住了天，
大青树盖住了地；
太阳看不见了，
月亮看不见了，
白昼变成了黑夜。
尖收倒在地，
化作“哒嘟哒”①。
地下漆黑一片，

① 哒嘟哒：一种夜鸟。

Jianshou cried three times everyday before it was dark,
she woke up three times every night before it was dawn.
Jianshou couldn't stand it anymore,
she was forced to pick up a begging stick,
and left home with tears running down her face.

She begged for food from the mountains to the seashore where rivers came together,

and from the seashore to the mountains where rivers originated.

One day, Jianshou came to the Amu Mountain,
where she saw a vast and boundless field in front of her.
The field's water drain outlet was wide,
so Jianshou crossed it with the help of her begging stick.
After she crossed the water outlet,
her begging stick took root,
and suddenly turned into a big green tree.

The big green tree shaded the sky
and covered the earth with darkness;
The sun became out of sight,
and so was the moon,
days turning into dark nights.
Jianshou fell to the ground,
and became a "daduda"①.
The earth was covered in such darkness,

① daduda: a nocturnal bird.

不知东边在哪方，
不知西边在哪方，
人有眼睛像没有眼睛一样。
人们把火把绑在牛角上犁田，
人们把火把拴在羊角上犁地，
可是栽下的庄稼不会长，
栽下的秧苗不会结谷子。

沉沉的黑夜无尽头，
世上的人们难忍受，
男女老少跪在地，
苦苦向天神哭诉：
“仁慈的莫米呀，
你为何把太阳月亮收起，
我们活不下去了，
快把太阳月亮放出来。”

男人的喉咙哭哑了，
女人的眼泪哭干了，
可是莫米没有回音，
太阳月亮还是出不来。

太阳到哪里去了？
月亮到哪里去了？
世上的人们一起商量，
决定派百兽到树顶瞧瞧，
找回太阳和月亮，
寻回生存的光明。

no one could tell where the east was,
or where the west was.
People had eyes, but it was like they didn't.
People tied torches to the cattle's horns to plow,
and to the ram's horns to plow,
but the crops they planted would not grow,
and the seedlings they planted would not yield grains.

The dark night had no end,
and people in the world could not bear it.
Men and women, young and old knelt on the ground,
crying their hearts out to plead to the god of heaven:
"Merciful Momi,
why did you take the sun and moon away?
we can't live like this,
so please sent the sun and the moon out."

Men shouted till their throats were sore,
and women cried till their tears were dry
but Momi didn't respond,
and the sun and the moon didn't come out.

Where did the sun go?
where did the moon go?
People in the world came together
and decided to send the animals to take a look at the tops of trees,
to see how they could get the sun and the moon back
to bring the light of life back.

第一次派出灵巧的猴子，
猴子磨破肉皮爬上树顶；
原来天还是晴朗，
日月星辰仍旧发光。
贪玩的猴子呀，
忘记主人的嘱咐，
三年不转路，
一去不回音。

人们又派出机灵的松鼠，
松鼠使尽力气爬上树顶；
原来天还是晴朗，
日月星辰仍旧发光。
松鼠被太阳迷住，
高兴得在树枝上跳舞；
贪玩的松鼠呀，
忘记主人的嘱咐，
三年不转路，
一去不回音。

人们又派出能飞的野鸡，
野鸡七天飞到树顶；
原来天还是晴朗，
日月星辰仍旧发光。
野鸡被美景迷住了，
放开嗓子在树上啼鸣；
贪玩的野鸡呀，
忘记主人的嘱咐，

They first sent the nimble monkeys,
who climbed their skin raw to get to the tops of the tree:
They found the sky was still clear,
with the sun, the moon and the stars still shining.
But the monkeys were too fond of playing
to remember the task given by their masters.
They didn't return for three years,
and no one ever heard from them again.

They then sent the smart squirrels,
who climbed up to the tops of trees with all their strengths:
They found that the sky was still clear,
with the sun, the moon and the stars still shining.
The squirrels were fascinated with the sun,
dancing happily on the branches;
They were also too fond of playing
to remember their mission entrusted by their masters.
They didn't return for three years,
and no one ever heard from them again.

People next sent pheasants that could fly,
who flew for seven days and got to the tops of the trees:
They found that the sky was still clear,
with the sun, the moon and the stars still shining.
The pheasants were mesmerized by the beautiful scenery,
singing at the top of their lungs on the trees;
They were too fond of playing
to remember their job given by their masters.

三年不转路，
一去不回音。

人们又派出飞得最快的蝙蝠，
蝙蝠像箭一样飞到树顶；
原来天还是晴朗，
日月星辰仍旧放光。

蝙蝠被太阳刺瞎了眼睛，
爬在树枝上不动，
三年不转路，
一去不回音。

日子一年一年过去了，
人们望穿了双眼。
请来燕子又去打听，
并向它许下了重愿：
“燕子呀！
你快去快飞回，
想尽办法查明原因，
来日人间得到光明，
让你与人类住一间房！”

三日不到燕子飞回，
把喜讯告诉人们：
“树上边天气晴朗，
日月星辰放光明。”

They didn't return for three years,
and no one ever heard from them again.

Again, they sent bats that flew fastest,
those bats flew up to the tops of the trees like arrows:
They found that the sky was still clear,
with the sun, the moon and the stars still shining.

But they were blinded by the sun,
lying on the branches, motionless.
They didn't return for three years,
and no one ever heard from them again.

Year after year,
people strained their eyes to find some reply so eagerly that their eyes hurt.
They invited swallows to inquire again,
and made a promise to them:
"Swallows!
Go and return quickly,
and try your best to find out the cause.
When the world gets the light again,
we let you live with people!"

Within three days, the swallows returned
with the good news:
"It was clear above the treetops,
with the sun, the moon and the stars still shining."

人们问燕子，
为哪样光照不到地上？
燕子只顾欢喜，
忘记查原因，
“吱吱”地说了半天，
一样原因也说不明。

人们又请蜜蜂去查看，
并向它许下了重愿：
“金蜂呀！
你快去快飞回，
想尽办法查明原因，
来日人间得到光明，
给你筑巢挂屋檐！”

三日不到蜂飞回，
向人们献了一个巧计：
“是树叶挡住了日月，
射穿树叶见光辉！”

各族兄弟围拢来，
推举仆拉①猎手阿戛：
“勇敢的阿戛，
你是世间最神的射手，
快握起奶桑木做的弯弓，
快扎上细牢的麻线，

① 仆拉：彝族一个支系的自称。

People asked swallows,
why couldn't the light shine on the earth?
The swallows were so happy
that they forgot to find out the reason.
Chirping for a long time,
they couldn't tell the reason.

People again asked the bees to check it out
and made a promise to them:
"Golden bees!
Go and return quickly,
and do your best to find out the cause.
When the world had the light again,
we let you build your nests under the eaves!"

Within three days, the bees flew back,
with a clever idea for the people:
"It is the leaves that block the sun and the moon,
so you can shoot through the leaves and then see the light!"

Brothers of all ethnic groups gathered around,
and elected hunter Ajia of Pula①:
"Brave Ajia,
You are the most astonishing archer in the world,
now you can hold the bow made of mulberry,
fasten the thin and durable flax thread,

① Pula: the name a group of Yi people given to themselves.

快配上最好的利箭，
施展出你高强的本领。”

千只眼不眨，
齐望阿戛的弩箭；
万颗心屏住，
想着阿戛的弓弦。

阿戛拉满弓弦，
弩箭飞出似闪电，
一声“轰隆”巨响，
一张牛皮大的树叶落下地。
人们见到一线阳光，
欢呼声震响山冈。

九十九寨的哈尼，
九十九寨的彝家，
九十九寨的汉人，
九十九寨的傣家……
大家聚拢来商量，
要砍倒大树见日月。

九千人拿刀砍，
九千人用斧劈，
九千人拉大锯，
九千人用凿子凿，
各族兄弟齐心合力，
像林中的老藤扭在一起；

match it with the sharpest arrow in the best quality,
to show us your extraordinary skill."

Thousands of eyes never blinked,
all gazing at Ajia's arrow,
and tens of thousands of people held their breath,
thinking about Ajia's bowstring.

Ajia pulled the bowstring to its limit,
and shot the arrow that flew out like lightning.
With a loud "boom",
a leaf as large as a piece of cowhide fell to the ground.
People then saw a ray of sunlight,
and their cheers echoed everywhere on the hills.

The Hani people from ninety-nine villages,
the Yi people from ninety-nine villages,
the Han people from ninety-nine villages,
and the Dai people from ninety-nine villages...
gathered together and decided
they must cut down the big tree to see the sun and the moon.

Nine thousand people cut it with knives,
nine thousand people chopped it with axes,
nine thousand people sawed it with large saws,
and nine thousand people chiseled it with chisels.
Brothers of all ethnic groups worked together,
like the old vines in the forest twisted together;

汗珠滚落汇成小河，
砍树的叮当声传百里。

日头落下山，
大树砍出一道口。
大伙心想只要砍几日，
大树就会倒在地；
可是明日一早起来看，
树上的斧口又长齐了。

二日砍，
三日砍，
砍了七天都一样：
白天大树见裂口，
明天起来一看无缝隙。

遮天大树没有砍倒，
背来的粮食吃完了。
人们都回去背粮食，
留下一个傣家守工具。

这个傣家人，
睡在树旁一个石洞里，
到了夜半三更时，
一阵说话声把他从梦中吵醒，
他竖起耳朵仔细听，
原来是守林的鬼神在议论：

their sweat rolled down and formed a stream,
and the thump of tree-cutting spread hundreds of miles away.

By sunset,
they made a crack on the big tree.
They all thought it would take just a few days
for the big tree to fall to the ground;
but next morning they saw,
the crack on the tree was no more.

They cut it a second day,
a third day,
but all seventh days were the same:
During the day, the big tree showed the crack,
but next morning the crack disappeared.

The sky-shading big tree wasn't cut down,
but the food they brought with them was eaten up.
People went back to fetch more food,
leaving only a Dai person to guard the tools.

This Dai person
slept in a stone cave by the tree.
At midnight,
He was awakened by the noise of people talking.
He listened carefully,
and found out that they were the spirit-guardians of the forest:

“不要怕，
不要怕，
不抹鸡屎砍不倒大树。”

大伙背着粮食转来了，
傣家把听到的秘密告诉大家。
大伙听了心里非常高兴，
派人回家背来鸡屎。

人们在刀口上抹上鸡屎，
砍树像切萝卜一样，
一刀更比一刀深；
千万刀砍下树摇晃，
大树随着一阵嘎嘎声，
天崩地裂倒下地。

遮天大树砍倒了，
阳光照到大地上。
百鸟飞出来唱歌，
百兽跑出来跳跃，
人们哟，
像过年过节一样欢乐。

遮天大树砍倒了，
人们细细数了数：
百丈高的大树，

"Fear not.

Fear not.

Without smearing the chicken droppings, they cannot cut down the big tree."

When other people returned carrying food on their backs,
The Dai person told them the secret he had overheard.
They were all very happy upon hearing the news,
and sent people home to fetch chicken droppings.

People then put chicken droppings on the edges of their knives,
and now chopping the tree was as easily as cutting turnips.
The crack got deeper and deeper with one chop after another.
After tens and thousands of chops the tree began to sway.
Then following a series of creaking sound,
the big tree fell with a bang that shook heaven and earth.

After the sky-shading big tree was cut down,
the sun shone on the earth.
hundreds of birds flew out to sing,
and all the animals ran out to dance.
People
felt so happy as if they were celebrating a holiday.

After the sky-shading big tree was cut down,
people counted the branches carefully:
The tree was hundreds of *zhang* tall,

共有十二杈，
后来人们把一年定为十二个月；
每一杈上长三十根树枝，
后来人们把一个月定为三十天；
每根树枝上长三百六十片叶子，
后来人们把一年定为三百六十天。

遮天大树砍倒了，
却把大地打碎了。
过去的大地，
是平平的一整块，
跟阿姆山一样高，
跟阿姆山山顶一样平。
大树倒下时，
把大地打成数不尽的坑坑洼洼，
这些坑坑洼洼哟，
后来变成了数不尽的江河湖海。

众人：萨——萨！

with twelve branches in total,

the number people later used to decide a year as having twelve months;

with thirty twigs on each branch,

the number people later used to decide a month as having thirty days;

with three hundred and sixty leaves on each twig,

the number people later used to decide a year as having three hundred and sixty days.

The sky-shading big tree was cut down,
but the crust of the earth was broken into pieces.
The surface of the earth in the past
was one flat piece,
as high as Mount Amu,
and as flat as its top.
When the big tree fell,
the earth was scared with innumerable potholes,
and oh, these potholes,
later became countless streams, rivers, lakes and seas.

Everyone: Sa—Sa!

五、阿扎多拉[①]

萨啦阿依——
天上没有太阳，
世间分不出白天黑夜来；
地上没有水，
田地里的庄稼不会栽；
世上没有火，
人类就不会发展到这一代。
红彤彤的火，
世间的人一个也离不开。

很古很古的时候，
我们的先祖连房子都不会盖，
到处乱睡觉，
人成了老虎豹子的饭菜。
那时候虎豹比人多，
宽宽的地上人不敢住，
冷天住在石洞里，
热天搬到树上住。

① 阿扎多拉：火的起源。

V. Azaduola[1]

Sala'ayi—
Without the sun in the sky,
the world would not be able to tell the day from the night;
without the water on the ground,
the crops in the fields would not have grown;
without fire in the world,
the humankind would not have developed to this generation.
The bright red fire,
no one in the world could live without.

In very, very ancient times,
our ancestors could not even build houses,
so they slept everywhere
and often became the foods for tigers and leopards.
At that time, there were more tigers and leopards than people.
so on the broad land, people didn't dare to stay.
In cold weather, they lived in the stone caves,
and on hot days, they moved onto trees.

① Azaduola: the origin of fire.

冷天住在石洞暖和和，
热天住在树上好凉快；
不怕热和冷，
不怕老虎豹子抬，
只是蟒蛇凶，
人天天要受到伤害。

我们的先祖，
住在石洞和树上日子难挨。
我们的先祖，
那时候不会栽棉花；
没有棉和线，
葛麻也不会采；
白天没有裤子穿，
晚上睡觉没有被子盖。

撕来芭蕉叶做衣裤穿，
捋来茅草做被子盖；
热天在茅草堆上睡，
冷天在茅草堆里埋。
只是芭蕉叶不牢，
身上很快被树枝戳坏。

我们的先祖，
穿芭蕉叶的日子艰难。
我们的祖先，
那时候谷子还不会栽；
不会养猪鸡，

The stone caves provided them shelters from the cold
and the trees cooled them off in hot days.
Not afraid of the cold or the heat,
or the attacks of tigers and leopards,
they were still unprotected from the vicious pythons
and were hurt every day.

Our ancestors,
had a hard time living in the caves and on the trees.
At the time,
they did not know how to plant cotton,
had no cotton and thread,
and did not know how to pick kudzu vine.
During the day, they had no pants to wear,
and at night, they had no quilts to cover them.

They tore the leaves from the banana trees to wear as clothes,
and collected thatches to cover themselves as quilts,
sleeping on top of the thatches on hot days,
and burying themselves in them on cold days.
But banana leaves were not strong enough to last,
and our ancestors were easily poked and bruised by twigs.

Our ancestors,
had a difficult time wearing banana leaves.
At that time,
they did not know how to plant crops,
or raise pigs and chickens,

生活也不会安排。
没有吃的，
大家上山把马鹿麂子逮；
马鹿麂子撵不着，
就到山上采野果野菜。

马鹿麂子味道虽然好，
有时候却几日逮不来；
遍山的野菜野果，
有时候也会全部枯败。
到了那时候，
人们就遭了大灾，
命小的就到阴间，
命大的就在世上留下来。

我们的先祖，
那时候还没有造出火来，
天冷的时候，
像猪一样乱草堆里埋；
逮来了麂鹿，
像豹子一样撕着吃生肉；
野菜采来了，
像牛马一样直往嘴里塞。

and didn't know how to plan ahead.
Without food to eat,
they just climbed up the mountains to catch red deer and moose,
and if they could not catch any,
they just picked wild fruits and wild vegetables in the mountains.

Although red deer and moose tasted good,
sometimes they couldn't be caught for quite a few days;
although wild vegetables and wild fruits were all over the mountains,
they sometimes could all wither away.
When these happened,
people suffered calamities,
the unlucky ones would die,
while the lucky ones barely survived.

Our ancestors,
at that time had not discovered how to make fire,
When it was cold,
they buried themselves in haystacks like pigs;
when they caught moose,
they tore and ate it raw like leopards;
when they picked wild vegetables,
they stuffed their mouths with them like cows and horses.

在那古老的年代，
整个大地一片青翠：
蕨蕨草像大青树一样高，
秆秆粗得有好几围；
肥壮的马鹿麂子，
成群地在树荫底下睡，
人们拿着石头和棍棒，
一起去把马鹿麂子围。

人们打死的马鹿麂子多了，
麂鹿吓得向遥远的地方隐退。
没有马鹿和麂子，
我们的先祖就只好搬家，
搬到有马鹿麂子的森林里；
马鹿麂子又跑了，
人们又把家搬一回。

马鹿麂子，
整天被人撵得不停腿，
顾不上吃一口青草，
顾不得喝一口清水，
日子过得不安宁，
天天向莫米控诉人的罪。

莫米被吵得发了怒，
丢下了几颗巨大的火雷。
无边的森林着了火，

In that ancient age,
the whole earth was covered with green:
ferns were as tall as big green trees,
and their stalks were so thick it took several hands to encircle and measure them;
herds of the fat red deer and moose,
slept in the shades of the trees,
so people with stones and sticks,
hunted the deer and the moose.

The more the red deer and the moose were hunted,
the farther away they retreated out of fear.
Without the red deer and the moose,
our ancestors had to move
to the forests with the red deer and the moose
who fled again,
and people had to move again.

The red deer and the moose,
chased by people, had to be on the run all day long,
without the time to have a bite of grass,
or a sip of water.
Their life became so frightening and distressed
that everyday they accused people of their crimes to Momi.

Momi was engaged by the onslaught of the accusations
and he dropped several huge fire bombs.
Thus the boundless forests caught fire,

火焰成了吃人的魔鬼，
老幼烧成了火炭，
枯木朽木烧成了白灰。

人们吓得胆战心惊，
急忙向遥远的地方逃避。
为了活命，
大家去把马鹿麂子追。
马鹿麂子逃向遥远的地方，
人们尾随紧紧在后边追。
马鹿麂子不停步，
人们也紧追不歇脚。

追到雷火烧过的林地，
烧死的麂鹿被乌鸦包围。
人们驱走了乌鸦，
撕碎了烧熟的麂鹿脚，
放到嘴里边一嚼，
觉得比吃生肉更有味，
比生肉好吃，
比生肉香脆。

我们的先祖，
有个叫司米锐，
吃了火烧肉，

and the flames became the devils that engulfed people.
The old and the young were burned into charcoals,
and the dry and rotten wood were burned into white ashes.

People were terror-stricken,
hurried to escape to the faraway places.
In order to survive,
they ran after the red deer and the moose.
However far the red deer and the moose fled,
the people followed them closely behind.
The red deer and the moose kept on running without stopping,
and people also chased after them without resting.

When people reached the woodland which was burned by the fire bombs,
they found crows surrounding the red deer and the moose killed by the fire.
They drove away the crows,
tore the burnt deer's feet to pieces,
and put them in the mouth and tasted them.
They found the burnt meant more flavored
more tasty,
and crisper than the raw meat.

Among our ancestors,
there was one Simirui,
who, after eating meat burnt by the fire,

感到肉味老实美，
知道火有很大用处，
就约大家一起去把火追。
找遍雷火烧过的地方，
寻遍了东南西北，
一点火也没有了，
只剩下一堆堆草木灰。

找火找不着，
就求莫米把火恩赐给人类。
男女老少，
不知给莫米磕头磕了多少回；
天上的莫米，
却一点火也不肯给。

司米锐的后代，
有个叫锐腿雷，
有天领着大家撵麂鹿，
麂鹿跑进深深的林子里，
林深草密虎豹多，
人们不敢再进林子追。
锐腿雷领着一伙人，
到山上滚石头把麂鹿催。

felt that it was really delicious,
realized that fire was very useful,
and gathered people to get fire.
They looked everywhere that had been burnt by the fire bombs,
and in all the four directions,
but they found no trace of fire,
only piles of plant ashes.

Since they failed to find fire,
so they pleaded to Momi to give fire to them as a gift.
Men and women, old and young,
kowtowed to Momi no one knows how many times,
but Momi in heaven,
wouldn't give them any fire.

Among the descendants of Simirui,
there was a Ruituilei.
One day when he led others to chase moose,
the moose ran deep into the woods,
where there were dense trees, thriving grass, many tigers and leopards.
So people out of fear would not go into the woods.
Ruituilei led some people
up the mountains and rolled stones down to force the moose out.

我们的先祖锐腿雷，
抱来一大块石头亮又白，
用力往山下一滚，
山坡上冒起了一大堆尘灰。
白石头狠狠砸在一棵树干上，
震得大地抖了抖；
干树冒起了青烟，
干树起火红焰飞。

见到红彤彤的火，
大家立即往地上跑，
感谢天上的莫米，
把火赐给了人类。
大家笑哈哈，
紧紧围住锐腿雷，
夸他求来了莫米的火，
称赞他有无穷的智慧。

马鹿麂子顾不着了，
大家跑去看火堆；
大火烧得旺，
大家都感到非常欣慰。
大家齐动手，
搬来干柴直往火里堆；
野火烧过了，
地上留下了火一大堆。

Our ancestor Ruituilei
found a big rock, bright and white,
gave it a hard push down the mountain,
and started the smokes of dust on the hillside.
The white rock smashed hard on one tree trunk,
shaking the earth;
the dry trunk gave out some blue smoke,
and some red flying flames from the dry trunk on fire.

Seeing the red fire,
everyone immediately started running down towards the ground.
They expressed gratitude to Momi in heaven
for giving the fire to the humankind.
Everyone laughed heartily
and stood around Ruituilei,
praising him for getting the fire from Momi,
and for having infinite wisdom.

No one worried about the red deer and the moose at this point,
and everyone ran to see the fire.
The fire was burning brightly,
which made everyone content.
They all pitched in,
bringing dry firewood and feeding it to the fire;
the wildfire burnt itself out,
but it left a lot of fires on the ground.

天天往火里堆干柴，
大大的火堆日日火焰飞。
人们白天上山撵麂鹿，
晚上在火堆里烧麂鹿腿。
烧熟的麂鹿肉，
大家吃着非常有味，
吃到肚子里，
香透了心和肺。

天天往火里添干柴，
大大的火堆日日火焰飞。
凶恶的蟒蛇不敢来，
残暴的虎豹也不敢来追。
黑漆漆的夜晚，
人就躺在火堆周围，
个个睡得热乎乎，
人人睡得甜又美。

人们有了火，
温暖的日子甜醉了心房，
吃得好来睡得香，
男人女人身体健壮。
女人生下小孩一大窝，
男人们个个喜洋洋，
小孩一天天长大，
地上的人越来越兴旺。

Everyday they threw dry firewood into the fire,
and the red flames kept flying from the big fire day after day.
People went up to the mountains to catch the red deer and the moose during the day,
and burnt the meat in the fire at night.
The cooked deer meat,
tasted very delicious to everyone.
The meat went into their stomach,
but made them feel content from the bottom of their heart.

Everyday they threw dry firewood into the fire,
and the red flames kept flying from the big fire day after day.
Vicious pythons didn't dare to come near,
and brutal tigers and leopards didn't dare to come after them.
During the dark nights,
they lay around the fire,
everyone sleeping a warm,
sweet and sound sleep.

Now that people had fire,
the warmth brought sweetness.
They ate and slept well,
men and women all in good health.
The women gave birth to lots of children,
and the men were all jubilant,
As the children grew up day by day,
the human population on the earth became bigger and bigger.

生活在地上的人们，
忘记了莫米的好心肠，
撵得麂鹿不祭献，
男女不分白天黑夜睡在一起。
天上的莫米发了怒，
把大水降到了地上；
红彤彤的火被浇熄了，
人们个个哭得泪汪汪。

没有红彤彤的火，
地上的人们遭了灾难，
麂鹿肉虽肥，
生撕硬嚼味道不甜香。
男女老少哟，
又成了老虎豹子的菜饭，
过着苦难的日子，
心田积满冰和霜。

男女老少齐跪下，
把麂子马鹿肉献上；
向莫米认罪过，
求莫米把红彤彤的火赏赐。

慈祥的莫米，
开口对人们讲：
红彤彤的火种，
早已放到了地上；
只要大家守规矩，

People living on the earth,
forgot Momi's kindness.
They offered no sacrifice to Momi after catching the moose,
and men and women slept together day and night.
Momi in heaven became very angry at them,
and brought the flood down to the earth,
the red flames were extinguished,
and people were all in tears.

Without the red fire,
people on earth were suffering a disaster.
Although the deer meat was fat,
it didn't taste sweet torn into pieces and eaten it raw.
Men and women, old and young
became the food of tigers and leopards once again.
Living in misery,
their hearts became frosty- and icy-cold.

Men and women, old and young, all knelt down
offering the red deer and the moose as the sacrifice,
contritely, they begged Momi
to give them fire again.

Merciful Momi,
spoke to people:
"The seed of the red fire
has long been given to the earth;
As long as everyone observes the laws,

天天把莫米记心房，
下功夫去寻找，
火种会闪出亮光。

人们牢记莫米的话，
到处去寻找火光，
寻遍了东西南北，
找遍了四面八方。
火种不得见，
人们都感到非常悲伤。

人们找不到火种，
像块石头压住了心房。
锐腿雷领着大家，
来到当年滚石头的山上，
寻来块块大白石，
不停地直朝山脚滚放；
山脚不见起火烟，
山脚不见起火光。

可怜的人们，
心里装着无限的希望，
又找来一块块大白石，
一次次直朝山脚滚放；
砸倒森林一大片，
砸得尘土满天飞扬；
一丝火烟也没起，

always keeps Momi in heart,
and tries hard to look for it,
the fire will shine to you.

People kept Momi's words in their mind,
and started searching for the shine of the fire everywhere.
They looked in the four directions,
and in all the places,
but the fire was still out of sight,
and people felt very sad.

Unable to find the fire,
people felt heavy at heart as if weighed down with a stone.
Ruituilei led everyone
back to the mountain where he rolled the rock down.
They found big white stones one by one,
and kept rolling them down toward the foot of the mountain,
but there was no smoke rising from the foot of the mountain,
no light of the fire at the foot of the mountain.

Poor people!
With great hope in their heart,
they found big white rocks one by one again,
and rolled them down towards the mountain foot again and again,
smashing down a large area of the forest,
and making the dust fly all over the sky.
But there was still not a trace of smoke,

一线火光也不见亮。
找不到火种心不死，
人们又连续把石头滚放，
滚了一天又一天，
滚了一趟又一趟。
可怜的人们，
眼睛直盯着山脚看，
仍然不见一丝火烟，
仍然不见一线火光。

劳作了一天心不死，
晚上又去把白石头滚放；
白石头顺着山坡一滚下，
山脚立即闪现出一道火光。
人们高兴了，
立即跑到山脚去观看；
看不到红红的火焰，
人们感到非常失望。

突然看见草丛里，
闪着微微的火光，
锐腿雷轻轻一抓，
原来火在一蓬绒草上；
莫米恩赐的火种，
原来放在这个地方。
可怜的人们，
心中升起了无限的希望。

and not a flash of fire.
Without finding the fire, they would not give up
and kept rolling rocks down along the mountain,
day after day,
one rock after another.
Poor people!
They kept their eyes on the mountain foot,
but there was still not a trace of smoke,
and not a flash of fire.

After a day's work they would not give up,
so they continued to roll the white rocks at night.
The moment the white rocks rolled down along the hillside,
a flash of fire appeared at the foot of the mountain.
People were so happy,
they immediately ran to the mountain foot to see.
But they didn't see the burning flame
and was quite disappointed.

Suddenly they caught the sight, in the grass
of some glowing embers.
Ruituilei touched it gently,
and found out that the fire was on top of a clump of fluffy grass.
The fire given by Momi,
turned out to be put here.
Poor people!
They had infinite hope again in their hearts.

大家扯来毛茸茸的草，
把珍贵的火种引上；
一团团的绒草，
使火烧得越来越旺。
突然腾起了火焰，
闪出了亮亮的火光。
大家又搬来一堆堆干柴，
把火引到大大的干柴堆上。

大火燃起来了，
火光照亮了四面八方。
蟒蛇吓得躲起来了，
虎豹不敢再到人身边。
男女老少，
睡着心里暖洋洋；
火烧麂鹿肉，
吃得嘴里肚里处处香。
红彤彤的火，
是人类生存的希望。
不能再让火浇灭，
不然人又要遭受祸殃；
把火搬回石洞里，
添上干柴把火烧旺，
用烧出来的火灰，
把火种好好埋藏。

People all pulled some fluffy grass,
to be lit by this precious fire.
One clump of fluffy grass after another
made the fire stronger and stronger.
Suddenly the flame rose up,
and flashed with bright light.
They then gathered piles of dry wood
and brought the fire to the big piles of dry wood.

When the big piles of dry wood started burning,
the firelight shone in all directions.
The pythons hid themselves out of fear,
and tigers and leopards were kept away from people from then on.
Men and women, old and young,
slept in warmth and content.
The burnt deer meat,
was delicious to their taste and satisfying to their stomach.
The red fire,
was the hope of people's survival.
They couldn't let it be doused again,
and couldn't let humans suffer again.
They brought the fire back to the stone caves,
added dry woods to let it burn strong
and used the burnt ashes
to store the fire seed.

人在搬家时，
首先不忘把火种带上；
到了新住处，
要先把火引着烧旺。
从今以后哟，
祖先就靠小小的火塘，
一代又一代，
把火传到了我们手上。

众人：萨——萨！

Whenever people moved,
they would first remember to bring the fire seed along.
When they arrived at the new places,
they would first ignite the fire and make it burn strong.
From then on,
our ancestors relied on the small fire pits,
generation after generation,
to pass the fire down to us.

Everyone: Sa—Sa!

六、阿匹松阿[①]

萨啦阿依——
遥远的天边，
有三块宽宽的平地：
开头一块是白的，
中间一块是花的，
下面一块是红的。

那时有三棵大树，
分别长在三块平地上：
开头一棵是白的，
中间一棵是花的，
下面一棵是红的。

三棵大树上，
开着三朵老实好看的花：
开头一朵是白的，
中间一朵是花的，
下面一朵是红的。

---

① 阿匹松阿：哈尼族传说中的能人，包括头人、工匠和贝玛。

Ⅵ. Apisong'a[1]

Sala'ayi—
In a place far away,
there were three pieces of broad flat land:
the first one was white,
the middle one, multicolored,
and the last one, red.

At that time, there were three big trees there,
each growing on one piece of the flat land:
the first tree was white,
the middle one was multicolored,
and the last one was red.

On the three big trees
there were three very beautiful flowers in bloom:
the first one was white,
the middle one was multicolored,
and the last one was red.

① Apisong'a: known as the capable people in Hani legends, including headman, craftsman and Beima.

三朵花上有三个窝，
三个窝里有三个蛋：
开头一个是白的，
中间一个是花的，
下面一个是红的。

三个蛋越看越神奇，
人们不知道是什么蛋，
有人问寨中放牛的小孩：
“在遥远的天边，
有三个不同色的蛋，
一个是白的，
一个是花的，
一个是红的，
知不知哪个是哪样蛋？
知不知会认蛋的人在哪里？”

放牛的小孩看看天边，
惊奇地睁大了眼睛，
像水牛甩尾一样把头摇，
连声说不知道。

又问放鸭的小孩：
“在遥远的天边，
有三个不同色的蛋，
一个是白的，
一个是花的，

The three flowers held three nests,
which had three eggs:
the first one was white,
the middle one was multicolored,
and the last one was red.

The more the villagers looked at the three eggs, the more amazed they felt,
knowing not what kind of eggs they were.
Someone asked a cowherd boy in the village:
"In the place far away,
there are three different colored eggs,
a white one,
a multicolored one,
and a red one.
Do you know what kind of eggs they are?
or do you know someone who knows?"

The cowherd looked towards the horizon,
widening the eyes in amazement,
shaking the head like a buffalo wagging its tail,
and kept saying that he didn't know.

They then asked a duck herding child:
"In the place far away,
there are three different colored eggs,
one white,
one multicolored,

一个是红的，
知不知哪个是哪样蛋？
知不知会认蛋的人在哪里？”

放鸭小孩看了看天边，
惊得张大了嘴巴，
像风吹树梢一样把头摇，
连声说认不得。

又问寨中的老人：
“在遥远的天边，
有三个不同色的蛋，
一个是白的，
一个是花的，
一个是红的，
知不知哪个是哪样蛋？
知不知会认蛋的人在哪里？”

寨中的老人一听，
高高兴兴地说：
“那是三个神蛋，
装着三种能人，
只要拿回蛋来抱，
白蛋会抱出头人来，
花蛋会抱出贝玛来，
红蛋会抱出工匠来。”

and the last red.
Do you know what kind of eggs they are?
or do you know someone who knows?"

The child looked towards the horizon,
opening the mouth wide in amazement,
shaking the head like the tree-tip blown by the wind,
and kept saying he had no idea of them.

They then asked the elderlies in the village:
"In the place far away,
there are three different colored eggs,
one white,
one multicolored,
and the last red.
Do you know what kind of eggs they are?
or do you know someone who can recognize the eggs?"

The elderlies
replied happily:
"Those are three sacred eggs,
which had in them three kinds of capable people.
Simply bring them back and let them hatch,
and there will be a headman from the white egg,
a Beima from the multicolored egg,
and a craftsman from the red egg."

拿回三个神蛋，
请大公鸡来抱，
抱了一百天，
神蛋冷阴阴，
抱死抱活不裂壳，
公鸡再也不敢抱了。

请老母鸡来抱神蛋，
母鸡抱了一百天，
神蛋没有一点热气，
左抱右抱不裂壳，
母鸡吓得不敢再抱了。

男人抱过了，
女人抱过了
狗也抱过了，
猫也抱过了，
鹅也抱过了，
鸭也抱过了，
神蛋还是冷阴阴，
神蛋还是不裂壳。

请教寨中的老人，
老人抬头指指天：
“三个神蛋天上来，
要请天上的太阳月亮抱。”

The villagers brought the three sacred eggs back,
and invited big roosters to hatch them,
but after a hundred days,
the eggs were still cold,
and no matter how hard they tried, the eggshells would not crack.
The roosters dare not continue.

They then invited old hens to hatch them
but after a hundred days,
the eggs were still not warm at all,
and no matter how hard they tried, the eggshells would not crack.
The hens were too scared to try again.

The men tried to hatch the eggs,
followed by the women,
the dogs,
the cats,
the geese,
and the ducks,
but the eggs were still cold
and uncracked.

They then asked the elderlies in the village,
who looked up and pointed to the sky:
"The three sacred eggs came from heaven,
so you have to invite the sun and the moon to hatch them."

太阳和月亮，
轮流抱神蛋：
白天太阳抱，
晚上月亮抱，
足足抱了九十天，
神蛋开始裂壳了。

三个神蛋抱出来了：
白蛋抱出来了，
花蛋抱出来了，
红蛋抱出来了。
一个不同一个，
三个蛋抱出三种能人。

头人从白蛋里抱出来，
声音像打雷一样响；
贝玛从花蛋里抱出来，
有撮鸡毛挂在嘴角上；
工匠从红蛋里抱出来，
声音像拉风箱爆火花一样。

头人的名字叫龙波阿优①，
长得高大又神采；
贝玛的名字叫龙斗阿沙②，

① 龙波阿优：哈尼族传说中的第一个首领。
② 龙斗阿沙：哈尼族传说中的第一个贝玛。

Now the sun and the moon
took turns to hatch the eggs:
the sun during the day
and the moon at night,
for exactly 90 days.
The sacred eggs started to crack.

The three sacred eggs were hatched:
the white one,
the multicolored one,
and the red one.
Different from one another,
three kinds of capable people were hatched out of the three eggs.

The headman was hatched out of the white egg,
with a sound as loud as thundering;
the Beima was hatched out of the multicolored egg,
with a chicken feather hanging from the corner of his mouth;
The craftsman was hatched out of the red egg,
with a sound like that of the bellows and firecrackers together.

The name of the headman was Longbo'ayou①,
and he was tall and handsome.
The name of the Beima was Longdou'asha②,

---

① Longbo'ayou: the first headman in Hani legends.

② Longdou'asha: the first Beima in Hani legends.

世上数他记性最好；
工匠的名字叫龙奴阿收①，
两手粗壮心灵手巧。

头人住在哪里？
在仰者城②的金殿上。
贝玛在哪里讲道理？
寨边长铁线草的路旁。
工匠在哪里传手艺？
寨门前有红土的地方。

头人分三等，
一等跟一等不一样：
一等头人头戴金帽子，
身穿长长的红衣裳，
出出进进坐大轿，
仰者城里很威风；
二等头人头戴银帽子，
身穿长长的黑衣裳，
出出进进骑大马，
培包③镇上有随从；
三等头人头戴铜帽子，

---

① 龙奴阿收：哈尼族传说中的第一个女工匠。
② 仰者城：哈尼族传说中的地名。
③ 培包：哈尼族传说中的城镇名。

and he had the best memory in the world.
The name of the craftsman was Longnu'ashou①,
and she had two strong hands and was skilled and smart.

Where would the headman live?
He settled in the Golden Palace of the Yangzhe City②.
Where would the Beima preach?
It would be by the road with the clematis grass and alongside the village.
Where would the craftsman impart skills?
It would be on the ground of the red clay in front of the village.

Some headmen were organized in three divisions,
which differed from one another:
first-class headmen wore gold hats
and long red robes.
They came and went in big sedan chairs,
looked at with prestige in the Yangzhe City.
Second-class headmen wore silver hats
and long black robes.
They came and went riding horses,
attended by servants in the Peibao③ Town.
Third-class headmen wore copper hats

① Longnu'ashou: the first female craftsman in Hani legends.
② Yangzhe City: name of a place in Hani legends.
③ Peibao: name of a town in Hani legends.

身穿长长的黑衣裳，
走路拄一根手杖，
窝龙龙坡、龙姿龙巴①查访。

工匠分三等，
一等跟一等不一样：
头等工匠手艺高，
炼铜炼铁倒犁花，
手拿弯尺和墨斗，
盖新房时立柱子；
二等工匠有办法，
打制锄头斧子和镰刀，
手拿斧子和锯子，
砍倒大树锯成板；
三等工匠手灵巧，
砍倒竹子树，
织出筛子、簸箕和背箩，
编制纸人和纸马。

自从世间有头人，
天天给人断事情，
吵闹打架的事少了，
抢人杀人的事少了；
地方管得平平的，
百姓好吃好在了。

---

① 窝龙龙坡、龙姿龙巴：分别为哈尼族传说中的地名。

and wore long black robes.
They each walked with a staff,
inspecting Wolong Longpo and Longzi Longba ①.

Some craftsmen were also organized into three divisions
which differed from one another:
First-class craftsmen were highly skilled,
smelting copper and iron for making plows,
and, with bendable rulers and ink markers in hands,
they erected pillars and built new houses.
Second-class craftsmen were resourceful,
making hoes, axes and sickles,
and, with axes and saws in hands,
they cut down big trees and made boards out of them.
Third-class craftsmen were dexterous,
cutting down bamboo trees
weaving sieves, winnowing fans and backpacks,
and making paper-men and paper-horses.

Ever since the headman came,
he arbitrated and solved problems for the villagers every day;
Quarrels and fights became fewer and fewer,
so did robberies and murders.
The villagers lived was well-managed,
and the villagers lived and worked in peace and with contentment.

① Wolong Longpo and Longzi Longba: both places in Hani legends.

人们为了谢头人，
把最俏的女人送给他做老婆，
把最贵重的东西送给他用，
把最好吃的东西拿给他享受。

自从世间有贝玛，
天天给人驱鬼治病。
他用黄泡刺挡住寨门，
用灶灰堵住路口。

魔鬼害怕了，
躲到深山悬崖里；
寨子不闹鬼了，
生病的人少了，
生出来的小娃长得大，
年纪大的老人活得长。

人们为了感谢贝玛，
把肉多的鸡腿牛腿送给他，
把白米和银子送给他，
把新布送给他。

自从世间有了工匠，
天天给人们做活计，
让人们有了铜铁做活省力气，
有了各种工具好栽田种地，
有了房子不怕风吹雨打，
百姓好吃好在过日子。

To thank the headman,
the villagers sent the most beautiful women to be his wife,
the most valuable things for him to use,
and the most delicious foods for him to enjoy.

Since the Beima came,
he drove away evil spirits and healed the villagers every day.
He blocked the village gates with the throng plants growing yellow berries,
and blocked the roads with ashes from the stoves.

The devils were scared
and hid themselves in the canyons of the remote mountains;
The village was not haunted any more
and fewer villagers got sick.
The newborns got to grow up
and the elderlies lived longer.

To thank the Beima,
the villagers gave him fat chicken legs and cattle legs,
white rice and silver,
as well as the newly-made cloths.

Ever since the craftsman came,
he worked every day for the villagers.
With the copper and iron, work was made easier;
With various tools, farming was made easier;
With houses to live in, life was sheltered from the elements.
The villagers lived and worked in peace and with contentment.

人们为了感谢工匠，
拿酒拿肉给他吃，
送谷送米养他的儿女，
拿出心来待工匠。

头人、贝玛和工匠，
一起生一起长的亲兄弟，
和和气气管人间，
百姓无灾无难安居乐业。

不知过了多少年，
不知过了多少代，
人们的心开始臭起来，
把头人、贝玛和工匠怨恨，
认为人间无灾难，
白白养活他们划不着。
村村寨寨吹起牛角号，
赶走了头人、贝玛和工匠。

头人赶走了，
人间出了大小事情没人断。
不知过了多少天，
不知过了多少年，
人们互相吵架打起来，
人们互相争斗杀起来。

To thank the craftsman,
the villagers gave him meat and wine,
grains and rice to help raise his children,
treating them kindly.

The headmen, Beima and craftsmen,
the three brothers, were born and growing up together.
They were friendly in managing the villages,
so that the villagers lived and worked in peace and with contentment without any disaster.

After many years,
or many generations,
the villagers had a change of heart,
resenting the headman, Beima, and craftsman.
They figured if the villages was free from disasters,
then it was not worth the effort to provide for them.
They blew the horns from one village to another
and drove away the headman, Beima and craftsman.

Without the headman,
the problems in the villages, big or small, were not arbitrated.
After many days,
and many years,
the villagers began to quarrel with one another,
to fight with and kill one another.

没有头人来坐堂，
一个管不着一个，
地方像冬天的大雾一样乱。

贝玛赶走了，
拦寨门的黄泡刺掉了。
不知过了多少天，
不知过了多少年，
成群魔鬼闯进寨子来吃人，
疾病和灾难像秋天的树叶一样落下来。

工匠赶走了，
寨门外的铁匠房倒了。
不知过了多少天，
不知过了多少年，
锄头斧子砍刀坏了没人修，
住的房子烂了没人盖，
人们不会栽田种地了，
人们不会安家过日子。

Without the headman in court to judge the cases,

no one listened to anyone else,

and the villages were as chaotic as the dense winter fog.

Without the Beima,

gone was the gate blockers of thorny plants growing yellow berries.

After many days,

and many years,

demons in large numbers broke into the villages to eat people,

and diseases and disasters fell upon them like autumn leaves.

Without the craftsman,

the blacksmith's workshop outside the villages collapsed.

After many days,

and many years,

the hoes, axes and choppers were broken but no one could repair them,

and the houses began to crumble but no one could rebuild them.

The villagers couldn't plow the fields or plant crops any more,

and couldn't live and work in peace and with contentment any more.

世间的人哟，
没有头人不会在，
没有贝玛不会在，
没有工匠不会在。
村村寨寨议论纷纷，
男人女人来商量：
要把头人请回来，
要把贝玛叫回来，
要把工匠找回来。

去问寨中的老人，
头人、贝玛、工匠在哪里；
老人摇摇头，
叹气不说话。

去问河坝的傣家，
头人、贝玛、工匠在哪里；
傣家摇摇头，
说他没见着。

去问做生意的汉人，
头人、贝玛、工匠在哪里；
汉人摇摇头，
说他没有遇着。

Oh, these villagers
could not live without the headman,
without the Beima,
without the craftsman.
All the villagers were talking,
and so all men and women together decided:
the headman must be invited back,
so must the Beima
and the craftsman.

They went to ask the elderlies in the village,
where to find the headman, Beima and craftsman;
The elderlies shook their heads
sighing without any words.

The villagers went to ask the Dai people living on the riverbank,
where to find the headman, Beima and craftsman;
The Dai people shook their heads,
saying that they had not seen them.

The villagers went to ask the Han tradespeople,
where to find the headman, Beima, and craftsman;
The Han people shook their heads,
saying that they had never run into them.

去问半山腰的彝家，
头人、贝玛、工匠在哪里；
彝家摇摇头，
说他没听说。

山鸡问过了，
白鹇问过了，
画眉问过了，
斑鸠问过了，
个个都说没见着，
个个都说不知道。

猴子问过了，
松鼠问过了，
野猪问过了，
马鹿问过了，
个个都说没遇着，
个个都说不知道。

人们包着冷饭到处找，
人们大声喊着到处叫，
找遍了宽宽的河坝，
听不到头人、贝玛、工匠的声音；
找遍了所有的半山腰，
看不到头人、贝玛、工匠的脚印；

The villagers went to ask the Yi people living half way up the mountains,
where to find the headman, Beima and craftsman;
The Yi people shook their heads,
saying they had not heard about their whereabouts.

They asked the pheasants,
the silver pheasants,
the babbling thrushes,
the turtledoves.
Every one of them said they had not seen them
or did not know anything about them.

They asked the monkeys,
the squirrels,
the wild boars,
the red deer.
Everyone said that they had never run into them,
and that they had no idea about them.

The villagers packed cold rice to look for them everywhere,
shouting their names everywhere.
They searched all over the wide riverbanks,
but they did not hear the voices of the headman, Beima and craftsman;
They searched all over the mountainside,
but they didn't see the footprints of the headman, Beima and craftsman;

找遍了所有的高山，
见不到头人、贝玛、工匠的影子。

人们的心像水浇着一样冷了，
人们的心像刺戳着一样难受了；
男人的嗓子哭哑了，
女人的眼泪哭干了。
恰恰这时候，
有只燕子从远处飞来。
人们问燕子：
“头人、贝玛、工匠在哪里？”

燕子站在树枝上，
歪着头对人们说：
“我飞遍了大地，
我飞过了大海，
头人、贝玛和工匠，
没听说过没见着。”

人们没有办法了，
苦苦请求燕子说：
“没有头人、贝玛和工匠，
我们一天也不会过日子；
求你可怜我们，
帮我们请回头人、贝玛、工匠来。”

they searched all over the high mountains,
but they did not find a trace of the headman, Beima and craftsman.

Their hearts were cold as if soaked in water,
painful as if pierced by thorns.
Men's throats were sore from crying
and women's tears were dried from crying.
Just then,
a swallow flew in from afar,
so they asked it:
"Where are the headman, Beima and craftsman?"

The swallow perched on a tree branch,
speaking to the villagers with its head tilted:
"I flew all over the earth,
and crossed the ocean,
but the headman, Beima and craftsman,
I have neither heard of nor seen them."

With no other means they could think of,
the villagers begged the swallow:
"Without the headman, Beima and craftsman,
we can't live our lives for even one day;
Please have pity on us,
and help us invite the headman, Beima and craftsman back."

燕子同情人们，
便飞去找头人、贝玛和工匠。
整整过了一年，
燕子飞回来告诉人们：
“头人、贝玛和工匠找着了，
住在遥远的天边边，
三弟兄栽田种地有吃有穿，
不愿回来让你们感到讨人厌。”

人们听了又悲又喜，
要求燕子发善心：
“你给我们带带路，
我们亲自去请他们。”

燕子心软了，
展开翅膀飞在前面带路；
人们跟在后面，
跨过了数不尽的江河，
翻过了数不清的高山，
足足走了一年，
来到三弟兄住的天边。

人们见到三个能人，
亲切地恳求他们说：
“尊敬的头人、贝玛和工匠，
过去是我们错了，
被泥巴糊住眼好坏不分，

The swallow sympathized with them,
so it flew out to look for the headman, Beima and craftsman.
After exactly a year,
the swallow returned and told the villagers:
"The headman, Beima and craftsman were found.
They lived in a place far away at the edge of the sky.
The three brothers were farming and had food and clothing
and didn't want to return to be a bother to you."

On hearing this the villagers were sad and happy,
begging the swallow for help:
"Would you please show us the way,
so that we can go to invite them ourselves."

The swallow was moved,
so, spreading the wings, it led the way.
The villagers followed it,
crossed countless rivers,
and climbed over countless mountains.
After a whole year,
they finally arrived at the edge of the sky where the three brothers lived.

When they saw the three capable men,
they pleaded to them sincerely:
"Respected headman, Beima and craftsman,
It is our fault in the past.
We were blind and couldn't tell good from bad,

没有你们我们不会过日子，
请你们回到我们那里去。”

头人听了笑了笑，
一句一句把话说：
“我当头人是莫米安排的，
我按照莫米的主意办事，
日日夜夜把心都操碎了，
你们心里却不喜欢；
现在我栽田种地日子好过，
我不愿当头人。”

贝玛听了皱着眉头，
一声一声把话说：
“我当贝玛也是莫米安排的，
我按照莫米的主意办事，
天天驱鬼治病忙得头昏眼花，
你们心里却嫌我；
这样的贝玛，
我一天也不会当。”

工匠听了眨眨眼，
一言一言把话说：
“我当工匠也是莫米安排的，
我按照莫米的主意办事，

but we see now that without you, we do not know how to live our lives,

so please come back to our place with us."

When the headman heard this, he smiled

and said slowly:

"It was Momi 's arrangement that I be the headman,

so I carried out Momi's plans.

I worked my heart out day and night,

but you didn't care for what I did;

Now I enjoy my farm life

and I don't want to be the headman anymore."

Hearing this, the Beima frowned

and said clearly:

"It was also Momi's arrangement that I be the Beima,

so I just carried out Momi's plans.

Ridding of evil spirits and curing diseases kept me so busy I was dizzy day and night,

but you insulted me;

such mistreatment

I would not subject myself to even for one day."

Then the craftsman, blinking his eyes,

said deliberately:

"It was also Momi's arrangement that I be the craftsman,

so I just carried out Momi's plans.

天天打铁盖房累得我吃睡不安，
你们心里却恨我；
这样的工匠，
我一天也不当。”

寨子人一起跪在地上，
流着眼泪苦苦哀求说：
“尊敬的头人、贝玛和工匠，
我们没有你们活不成，
要是你们不回去，
我们就跪在这里死也不起来。”

头人的眼泪淌出来了，
贝玛的鼻涕流出来了，
工匠的声音哭出来了，
三弟兄跟着寨子人回来了。

头人回来了，
天天忙着给人们断事，
不听话的人拿棍子打，
恶人拿刀杀。
大家规规矩矩过日子，
地方很快平定了。

贝玛回来了，
天天忙着给人们驱鬼治病，

Blacksmithing and building houses kept me so exhausted I couldn't' eat and sleep well day and night,

but you resented me;

Such abuse

I would not subject myself to even for one day."

All the villagers knelt in front of the three men,

begging earnestly in tears:

"Respected headman, Beima and craftsman,

we can't live without you.

If you don't go back with us,

we will kneel here until we die."

Moved, the headman was in tears;

the Beima's nose was running;

and the craftsman was sobbing.

The three brothers returned with the villagers.

After the headman returned,

he was busy adjudicating cases everyday.

The disobedient was punished with sticks,

and the wicked, with capital punishment.

Everyone behaved,

and the order was soon restored.

After the Beima got back,

he was busy dispelling devil spirits and curing the villagers everyday.

寨门挂上了黄泡刺，
路口撒上了灶窝灰。
魔鬼不敢闯进寨子了，
人们平平安安过日子。

工匠回来了，
天天忙着给人们打铁盖房子。
锄头斧子和砍刀打出来了，
人们欢欢喜喜栽田种地；
新新的房子盖起来了，
人们舒舒服服地安家。

众人：萨——萨！

Once again, the thorny plants growing yellow berries were hung on the village gates,

and the ashes from the stoves were sprinkled over the village roads.

The devil did not dare to break into the villages

and the villagers lived in peace and safety.

After the craftsman came back,

he was busy blacksmithing and building houses for the villagers everyday.

Hoes, axes and choppers were made

so that the villagers farmed happily.

New houses were built,

and the villagers settled down comfortably.

Everyone: Sa—Sa!

七、觉麻普德[1]

萨啦阿依——
远古的哈尼师厄[2]，
住着一家三个弟兄：
大哥叫觉麻，
二哥叫觉车，
三弟叫觉冲。

这里森林密得望不见天，
一年四季云雾腾腾，
野兽像蚂蚁一样多，
毒虫像树叶一样旺，
兄弟三人无法安身。

他们听说遥远的地方，
有块富饶的土地，
生出来的儿子力气大，
生出来的姑娘样子俏；

---

① 觉麻普德：一个叫觉麻的人建寨。
② 哈尼师厄：古地名，地址不详。

Ⅶ. Juema'pude[①]

Sala'ayi—
In the ancient Hanishi'e[②],
lived a family of three brothers:
The first brother Juema,
the second one Jueche,
and the third Juechong.

The forest where they were at first was too thick to see the sky,
with clouds and mists floating all year round.
Beasts were as many as ants,
and poisonous insects, as numerous as leaves.
The three brothers could not live there.

They heard that in a place far away
there was a piece of rich land,
where boys were born strong,
and girls were born pretty,

① Juema'pude: Juema, a person, built the village.

② Hanishi'e: name of an ancient place, today's location unknown.

土肥水好好栽田和地，
栽一年能吃两年；
芋头叶子比簸箕大，
一棚嫩草够七头牛吃。

弟兄三个离开森林，
去寻找这个好地方；
弟兄三人走了九天九夜，
来到了一个河坝。

河坝的谷米一年两熟，
河坝的泉水四季流淌；
可是吃了谷米发瘴气，
喝了泉水肚子疼，
指甲壳上看不见血色，
人的脸上没有亮光。

他们认出这里不是好地方，
又离开河坝去寻找。
他们走了九天九夜，
来到一块平地。

这里的山四季常绿，
这里的水天天流淌；
热风吹来给人营养，
凉风吹来人有血色。

where the soil was fertile, moist for farming,
and a year’s harvest could feed people for two years;
where the taro leaves were bigger than winnowing pans,
and a clump of tender grass was enough to feed for seven head of cattle.

The three brothers left the forest
to look for this good place.
They walked for nine days and nine nights
and came to a riverbank.

The rice on the riverbank could have two seasons a year
and the spring water on the riverbank flowed all year round;
But people got sick from eating the rice,
got stomachache after drinking the spring water,
their fingernails lost the color
and their faces darkened.

They realized it was not a good place
and left the riverbank to keep looking.
They walked another nine days and nine nights
and came upon a piece of flat land.

The mountains there were green all year round,
with the water flowing all day long;
the blowing warm wind nourished people
and the cool breeze gave them ruddy cheeks.

大哥觉麻停下来,
忙对两个弟弟说:
"这里是个好地方,
水好土肥好栽田地;
我们停下来吧,
再好好选个寨址安家。"

觉麻三弟兄停下来,
择了个吉祥的日子,
登上一座高高的山顶,
选一个安居乐业的寨址。

觉麻在山顶转去转来,
眼睛朝四周的山梁望去,
看见一条蜿蜒的河边上,
有一座衔着白云的梁子,
梁子上森林密密麻麻;
森林中间有块洼地,
洼地里清澈的龙潭,
像一块明亮的镜子。

觉麻高兴了,
觉麻看上了:
"这里是个好地方,
这里是个好寨址,
我们在这里建寨,
我们在这里安家。"

The first brother Juema stopped walking
and said to his two younger brothers in eagerness:
"This is a good place,
with plenty of water and fertile soil good for growing crops.
Let us not go any further
and choose a good place for the village and settle down here."

Juema and his brothers
chose an auspicious day,
and went to the top of a high mountain,
to pick a location for their village.

Juema walked around on the mountaintop,
looking at the mountain ridges around.
He saw, beside a winding river,
a ridge covered with clouds
and dense forests;
in the middle of the forest was a basin,
with clear Longtan springwater
like a bright mirror.

Juema was pleased
and decided they had found it:
"This is a good place,
a good location for the village
Let's build our village
and settle down here."

觉麻择了个最吉利的日子，
带着两个弟弟，
抬着斧子和锯子，
到山上挑选柱子。

雷打过的树不能要，
要了房子容易着火烧；
秃了顶的树不能要，
要了子孙后代不会发；
虫吃过的树不能要，
要了人会疾病多；
空心的树不能要，
要了房子盖得不稳扎。

先到东边山上找，
整个山林瞧过了，
挑过去挑过来，
林中所有的树木，
没有一棵如意的，
没有一棵合心的。

来到北边山上找，
转遍了整个山林，
挑过去挑过来，
林中所有的树木，
没有一棵如意的，
没有一棵合心的。

Juema chose a most auspicious day,
went with his two younger brothers,
carrying the axes and saws,
to get the timber in the mountains for building the house.

The trees that had been struck by lightning weren't wanted,
because they would make houses a fire hazard;
the trees with no leaves weren't wanted,
because they would not allow future generations to be prosperous;
the trees infested with bugs weren't wanted,
because they would cause people to have many diseases;
the hollow trees weren't wanted,
because they would not make the houses stable.

They first went to the mountain in the east,
looked everywhere,
picked carefully through
all the trees in the forests,
but they found not one that met their expectations,
not one that was satisfactory.

They then went to the mountain in the north,
looked everywhere,
picked carefully through
all the trees in the forests,
but they found not one that met their expectations,
not one that was satisfactory.

来到西边山上找，
转遍了整个山林，
挑过去挑过来，
林中所有的树木，
没有一棵如意的，
没有一棵合心的。

来到南边山上找，
转遍了整个山林，
挑过去挑过来，
挑过了林中所有的树木；
在一个朝阳的山坡上，
砍到了坚硬挺直的栗木柱。

择了个吉祥的日子，
到河边的山坡上割茅草。
做过雀窝的茅草不能要，
要了麻蛇会进家里来；
蛆虫吃过的茅草不能要，
要了耗子会来做窝；
绿茵茵的茅草不能要，
要了雨天会漏雨；
倒在地上的茅草不能要，
要了风天不挡风。

转来转去地找，
挑来挑去地选，
找遍了山山岭岭，

They went to the mountain in the west,
looked everywhere,
picked carefully through
all the trees in the forests,
but they found not one that met their expectations,
not one that was satisfactory.

They went to the mountain in the south,
looked everywhere,
picked carefully through
all the trees in the forests.
On a sunny hillside,
they got the hard and straight chestnut tree for the pillars.

They chose another auspicious day
to gather the thatches on the hillside by the river.
The thatches birds had used to make nests couldn't be used,
because they would attract snakes to the house;
the thatches infested with the maggots couldn't be used,
because they would lead mice to the house to dig their holes;
the fresh green thatches couldn't be used,
because they would leak when it rained;
the thatches that flopped on the ground couldn't be used,
because they couldn't keep out the wind when it blew.

They looked for thatches all around,
and picked them carefully one by one.
They climbed all over the mountainsides,

踩遍了沟沟洼洼，
在一面朝阳的山坡上，
割到了黄生生的茅草。

择了个吉祥的日子，
到箐沟割藤子。
鬼藤子①不能要，
要了容易引鬼进家来；
蛆虫吃过的藤子不能要，
要了地神不喜欢；
嫩藤子不能要，
要了扎不稳竹排；
挂着蛇皮的藤子不能要，
要了会吓着祖宗。

转来转去地找，
挑来挑去地选，
钻遍了每一条箐沟，
找遍了每一条冲冲，
在一条深深的箐沟里，
割到了牢牢的藤子。

择了个吉祥的日子，
到山坡上砍竹子。
做过蜂窝的竹子不能要，

① 鬼藤子：血藤。

walked all over the ditches and puddles
and got, on a sunny hillside,
the golden yellow thatches.

They chose again an auspicious day,
to cut rattan in the woody valley.
The *gui* rattan① couldn't be used,
because they were likely to bring ghosts into the house;
the rattan that was full of maggots couldn't be used,
because using them would offend the god of earth;
the tender rattan couldn't be used,
because they wouldn't fasten the bamboo rafts tight;
the rattan covered with sloughed snakeskin couldn't be used,
because they would scare the ancestors.

They looked for the rattan all around
and picked them carefully one by one.
They went through almost every valley,
searched almost every ditch.
and found, in a deep valley,
the very strong rattan.

They chose yet another auspicious day
to cut bamboos on the hillside.
The bamboos on which the hornets had built their nests were not wanted,

---

① *gui* rattan: the magnolia vine.

要了容易引豹子进家来；
断了尖尖的竹子不能要，
要了人命活不长；
开花的竹子不能要，
要了要败家产；
蛆虫吃过的竹子不能要，
要了人容易生疮。

转来转去地找，
挑来挑去地选，
找遍了每一蓬竹子，
踩遍了每一片竹林，
在朝阳的山坡上，
砍到了俏生生的竹子。

择了个吉祥的日子，
找一块平地打土基。
黑土不能要，
用黑土打出来的土基不方正；
白土不能要，
用白土打出来的土基不牢靠；
夹石子的土不能要，
用夹石子的土打出来的土基容易裂。

转来转去地找，
挑来挑去地选，

because they were likely to attract leopards into the house;
the bamboos with broken tips were not wanted,
because they would not let people live long lives;
the bamboos that had bloomed were not wanted,
because they would cause people to bankrupt;
the bamboos that had been damaged by maggots were not wanted,
because they would likely cause people to get sores.

They looked for bamboos all around
and picked them carefully one by one.
They looked through almost every bamboo clump,
walked through every bamboo forest,
and got, on the sunny hillside,
some graceful bamboos.

They chose another auspicious day,
to look for a flat land to make the clay foundation bricks.
Black dirt couldn't be used,
because it would not make the foundation bricks square and straight;
white dirt couldn't be used,
because it would not make the foundation bricks firm;
soil mixed with gravel couldn't be used,
because it would make the foundation bricks likely to crack.

They looked for it all around,
and searched for it carefully from one place to another.

踩遍了每一个山坡，
找遍了每一个冲沟，
在山脚的洼地上，
找到打土基的红土。

择了个吉祥的日子，
选个牢固的地基。
有洞的地基不能要，
要了雨天房子会崩塌；
走动的地基不能要，
要了以后房子会垮倒；
垭口上的地基不能要，
要了房子会被风吹掉；
冲沟沟里的地基不能要，
要了雨天会被洪水淹。
转来转去地找，
挑来挑去地选，
找遍了每一块土块，
踩遍了每一道坎坷，
在一块朝阳的山坡上，
选好了牢固的地基。

地基踩好了，
地基选定了。
杀只大红公鸡祭天地，
求天神地神保佑平安；
挖去松软的浮土，
平出平坦的地基。

They went through every hillside,
searched every gully,
and found, at the low land by the foot of the mountain,
the red dirt for the foundation bricks.

They chose another auspicious day,
to select a good location for a solid foundation.
The ground with holes was not wanted,
because it would cause the house to collapse when it rained;
the ground that could shift was not wanted,
because it would cause the house to fall down;
the ground on the narrow mountain pass was not wanted,
because it would let the house be blown away by wind;
the ground in the gully was not wanted,
because it would cause the house to be flooded when it rained;
They looked for it all around,
and searched for it carefully from one place to another.
They searched over every piece of land,
walked on every bumpy road,
and selected, on a sunny hillside,
the land for the solid foundation.

The foundation was chosen
and decided.
They sacrificed a red rooster to heaven and earth
and prayed to the gods of heaven and earth for protection.
Digging away the soft soil,
they then leveled out the flat foundation.

柱子砍来了，
茅草割来了，
藤子扯来了，
竹子砍来了，
土基打好了，
地基平好了，
要立柱子啰，
要盖房子啰。

择了最好的日子立柱子，
三个弟兄一起砌土基，
三个弟兄一起拴椽子，
三个弟兄一起铺茅草。
新新的房子盖好了，
立起三块石头做锅桩石，
拿来三把干干的柴块；
燃着的柴块暖烘烘，
灰蓝蓝的火烟升上天，
四面八方都知道这里安了寨子。
要使寨子有个好名声，
让好名声传到遥远的地方。

房子盖好了，
要找个好好的水井。
雨季才会冒水的龙潭不能要，
田地里滴下来的尾水不能要，

With the pillars ready,
the thatches ready,
the rattan ready,
the bamboos ready,
the foundation bricks ready,
and the foundation ready,
they were going to set up the pillars,
and build the houses.

They chose the best day to erect the pillars,
and the three brothers worked together to lay the foundation bricks,
to tie up the rafters,
and to lay the thatches.
After the new house was built,
they set up three rocks as the stake rocks;
They then brought three bundles of dried firewood,
let them burn with warmth
and with the gray-blue smoke rising to the sky,
to let people in all directions know the newly built village.
The brothers hoped for a good reputation for the village,
so that it is known even in distant places.

The house was built,
and they needed to find a good well.
The Longtan spring which only had water during the rainy season wasn't wanted,
nor was the water dripping from the end of the fields,

会冒浑水的龙潭不能要，
遍地浸出来的水不能要；
只要清清的龙潭水，
龙潭水是龙吐出来的。
龙吐出来的清泉水，
甘甜清凉最养人的心。
喝龙潭水长大的伙子，
个个勤劳勇敢有本事；
喝龙潭水长大的姑娘，
个个生得像花一样俏。

转来转去地找，
挑来挑去地看，
找遍了每一条冲冲，
踩遍了每一道山梁，
在寨边的洼地里，
找到了一眼清澈的龙潭。

挖去旁边的泥土，
抬来硬硬的石板，
把四周砌起来，
把龙潭围在中间。
水井修好了，
杀一只红公鸡祭献天地，
求天神地神好好保护龙潭，
一年四季都冒清清的泉水。

nor was the Longtan spring which could run muddy water,
nor was the water from the saturated ground.
Only the clear Longtan spring water was wanted,
because it sprang from the mouth of the dragon.
From the dragon came the clear spring water
that was sweet, cool and nourishing.
Every young man growing up on the spring water
was industrious, brave and capable;
every young women growing up on the spring water
was as beautiful as flowers.

They looked for it all around,
and examined carefully all the places.
They searched every gully,
walked through every ridge,
and found, on the low land by the village,
a clear Longtan spring.

They removed the mud around the fountainhead,
brought hard slates
and laid them around
the Longtan spring.
Now that the well was ready
they sacrificed a red rooster to the gods of heaven and earth,
praying to them for the protection of the Longtan spring
and for the clear spring water all year round.

寨头封起一片林，
世世代代不要砍；
安一座普玛做护寨神，
每年杀一次猪鸡敬献；
请求护寨神显灵，
保佑全寨人无灾无难，
保佑猪鸡不病不死，
保佑牛羊又肥又壮，
保佑年年风调雨顺，
保佑庄稼年年丰收。

寨边的草坪上，
建起玩乐的磨秋场。
砍来坚硬的栗木，
栽起永世不朽的磨秋桩。
每年六月矻扎①到了，
牵来肥壮的黄牛，
在磨秋场上杀翻；
点亮松明火，
门头挂上绿松枝，
男女老少敲锣打鼓，
迎接神仙威咀到寨上。

神仙威咀来了，
给寨子带来幸福和吉祥；

① 矻扎：哈尼族的一个传统游戏节目。

A part of the forest in front of the village was protected,
never to be cut;
a Puma was set up there as the guardian of the village,
sacrifices of pigs and chickens to be offered to it once a year,
they asked the guardian to
bless the villagers to be free from disasters,
bless the pigs and chickens to be free from deadly diseases,
bless the cattle and sheep to be fat and strong,
bless them all with good weather every year,
and bless the crops with good harvests year after year.

On the grassland beside the village
they set up the Moqiu park.
They found the hard chestnut woods
and erected Moqiu stakes that would stand forever.
Every June, when it was time for Kuzha①
people brought the fat cattle
to be butchered on the Moqiu playground;
they lit up the pine-wood torches,
hung the green pine branches from the top of the doors.
Men and women, old and young, beat drums and hit gongs
to welcome Fairy Weizui to the village.

When Fairy Weizui came,
he brought happiness and luck to the village;

---

① Kuzha: a traditional Hani game show.

神仙威咀骑着白马要走了，
全寨男女老少到磨秋场，
擂响地神听得见的牛皮鼓，
敲响天神听得见的铓锣，
跳起欢乐的鼓舞，
骑着磨秋升到天上，
欢送我们的神仙威咀，
骑着白马回到遥远的地方。

庄稼收完了，
黄生生的谷子收回来了；
杀翻肥肥的大猪，
踩好白白的糯米粑粑，
烧一甑香甜的焖锅酒，
宰杀大大小小的鸡鸭。
请天神来过新年，
请地神来过新年，
接回祖先来过年，
接回和祖宗不在一起的家人①来过年；
新的一年开始了，
一家人欢欢喜喜过几日。

① 指非正常死亡的人。

when Fairy Weizui was leaving on a white horse,

all men and women, old and young, of the village gathered at the Moqiu park

playing the cowhide drums that could be heard by the god of earth,

striking the gongs that could be heard by the god of heaven,

dancing joyfully to the sound of the drums,

and riding the Moqiu (Hani style seesaw) to the sky

to send off our Fairy Weizui,

who rode the white horse back to a distant place.

After the harvest,

the golden unhusked rice was in the barn;

fat pigs were butchered;

the white glutinous rice cakes were made;

a steamer of the sweet rice wine was brewed;

and chickens and ducks, big or small, were prepared.

They now invited the god of heaven to celebrate the New Year,

the god of earth to celebrate the New Year,

the ancestors back to celebrate the New Year,

the deceased family members not with the ancestors① to celebrate the New Year.

In the beginning of a new year,

family members would rejoice together for a few days.

① People who did not die a natural death.

要盖寨门了，
要给寨子安个大门了，
抬来大大的石头，
砍来坚硬的锥栗木。
寨门盖好了，
老人小娃有玩的地方了。

寨门盖好了，
寨门安好了，
把客人请进寨子来，
把恶人堵在寨门外。

寨门盖好了，
请来高能的贝玛，
把寨里的魔鬼驱出寨门，
把灾难和疾病赶出寨门；
砍来黄泡刺，
稳稳挂在寨门上，
把魔鬼挡在寨门外，
把灾难和疾病挡在寨门外。

寨门盖好了，
寨子建起来了。
房前屋后要栽上树：
寨脚的田坝栽杨柳，
寨脚的坡子上栽竹子，
寨门外边栽大青树。

Time to build the village gate,
the big village gate,
so large stones were gathered,
and hard chestnuts woods were cut.
Once the gate was built,
the elderlies and the youth could have a place to visit and to play.

The gate was now built;
it was built.
The guests were invited into the village,
and the wicked were kept out of it.

After the gate was built,
they invited the capable Beima,
to drive the devils out from the village gate,
to drive disasters and diseases out of the village gate.
They cut the thorny plants growing yellow berries
and hung them firmly on the gate
to keep the devils out of the village gate,
to keep disasters and diseases out of it.

The village gate was built,
and the building of the village was finished.
Trees must be planted in front of and behind house:
willows were planted on the riverbank at the foot of the village,
bamboos were planted on the hillside at the foot of the village,
and big green trees were planted outside the gate of the village.

寨子栽上了树木，
寨神心里老实喜欢，
天天守在寨子里。
寨子像大象筋拉着一样稳扎，
寨子像大象皮箍着一样牢固，
寨里的房子不会歪倒了，
寨脚的陡坡不会崩塌了。

觉麻三弟兄把寨子建起来，
寨子的名字叫麻密①。
觉车到各地建街子，
觉冲到别处建寨当首领，
觉麻留在麻密寨安家创业。
人一代一代繁衍，
世间的寨子一寨一寨建起来。

众人：萨——萨！

① 麻密：寨名。

The trees planted in the village
truly pleased the guardian of the village
who guarded the village dutifully every day.

The village was secure like it were pulled together by the elephant tendon

and safe like it were protected by walls of the elephant skin;
the houses in the village would not become crooked and fall

and the mud of the steep slopes at the foot of the village would not slide.

Juema and his brothers had built the village,
and they named it Mami①.
Jueche then went to build more streets everywhere;
Juechong went to build villages and became the village head;
and Juema stayed in Mami and started his own livelihood.
People multiplied generation by generation,
and villages in the world were build one after another.

Everyone: Sa—Sa!

---

① Mami: name of the village.

八、牡实米戛[1]

萨啦阿依——
天上有滴红彤彤的血，
忽然掉下大地。
血洒落在哪里？
洒落在寨子边的草坪上。
猪啊，请你不要去拱土，
也不要去踏草坪。
猪摇摇摆摆游出寨子，
天上的血沾在猪身上了。

狗啊，请不要去咬猪，
也不要乱叫。
狗冲出寨子咬猪，
天上的血沾在狗毛身上。

女人啊，请不要去打狗，
也不要发躁。
女人骂着打狗，
天上的血会沾到女人身上。

---

① 牡实米戛：天血掉落在地上，即生儿育女。

Ⅷ. Mushimiga[①]

Sala'ayi—
A drop of the red blood in the sky
suddenly fell to the earth.
Where did it fall?
It fell on the pasture by the village.
Pigs, please don't dig the earth,
and don't tread on the grass.
But the pigs strolled out of the village,
and now the heavenly blood got on the pigs.

Dogs, please don't bite the pigs,
and also stop barking.
But the dogs charged out of the village to bite the pigs,
and now the heavenly blood got on the dogs' hair.

Women, please don't hit the dogs,
and don't get impatient.
But the women scolded and hit the dogs,
and now the heavenly blood got on the women.

---

① Mushimiga: the blood of heaven fell on the earth, that is, giving birth to children.

寨中有人说：
“狗血抹在人身上，
血糊哩啦多腥气；
威咀看了不顺眼，
说还是赶快洗了吧！”

沾在人身上的血，
红得像朵大红花，
那不是猪血，
那不是狗血，
是人要发展兴旺的血。

不是黑头鸪尾下的毛发红，
是女人身上流出的血红亮；
不是园子里的桃子开花，
是血在女人们的身上开花。

不会开花结果的树不要栽，
能开花结果的树人喜欢；
果实累累的桃树人爱护，
会生儿育女的女人才值钱。

Some in the village said:
"The dog's blood smeared on people,
is too bloody and smelly;
Fairy Weizui would not like it,
so go and wash it off quickly!"

The blood on people
was red like a big red flower.
That was not pig's blood,
or dog's blood,
it was the blood that would let the people prosper.

It was not the red hair under the tail of the black-headed partridge,

but the red and bright blood flowing out of the women' bodies;

It was not the peaches in bloom in the garden,

but the blood that bloomed on the women's bodies.

Trees that could not blossom and bear fruit were not planted,

while trees that could blossom and bear fruit were preferred by people.

Just as the peach trees loaded with fruits were protected by people,

the women who could bear children were valuable.

我家的女人，
不像别人一样，
身子发冷发热，
脚瘫手软没有力气；
走路跟不上人家，
喘气不同别人，
吃饭没有滋味，
喝水也不清甜，
上山下田不爱做活计，
一天到晚没有精神；
她不是生病软绵绵，
是肚子里怀娃娃了。

娃娃怀两个月了，
一只手一只脚长出来了；
娃娃怀三个月了，
两只脚一只手长出来了；
娃娃怀四个月了，
两只脚两只手长出来了
……
娃娃怀了九个月，
像到时的花朵要谢，
像成熟的瓜果要落，
生娃娃的月份到了。

娃娃生出来了，
下地会哭三声了；

When a woman in a family
was unlike others—
her body felt now cold now hot,
her feet and hands weak,
and she couldn't keep up with others when walking,
breathed differently,
had no appetite for food
or water,
didn't want to work up the mountains or in the fields,
and felt listless all day long—
she was weak not because she was sick
but because she was expecting a baby.

When she was two-month pregnant,
the baby grew one hand and one foot.
When she was three-month pregnant,
the baby grew the other foot.
When she was four-month pregnant,
the baby grew the other hand.
…
When she was nine-month pregnant,
like flowers reaching full term would wither
and fruits reaching full term would fall,
the baby was due to be born.

When the baby was born,
it would cry three times:

脐带要割断下来了，
娃娃不能给冷着，
阿爹三天不要出门下田，
阿妈三天不要烧火煮饭。

生下一个孩子，
一家人都很高兴，
要煮糯米饭，
送给寨里的长老乡亲。

杀只鸡给取个名字，
给男孩取的名字，
要同阿爸名字连着叫；
给女孩取的名字，
不兴同阿爸连着叫，
愿的是孩子能平安长大。

抱在大腿上，
孩子会笑了，
会认阿妈了，
会认阿爸了，
像小山雀一样会叫了，
像小瓦雀一样会说话了。

在地上会爬着玩了，
摇摇晃晃地会走路了，
渐渐地会玩灰了；
一天一天地长大，

The umbilical cord would be cut,
and the baby would be kept warm;
the father didn't go to work in the fields for three days
and the mother didn't cook for three days.

To give birth to a baby
was a happy event for the whole family,
they would cook glutinous rice
to treat the fellow villagers, old and young.

They would butcher a chicken when naming the baby.
When naming a boy,
they connected the name to the father's;
when naming a girl,
they did not connect the name to the father's,
in hopes that the babies would grow up safely.

The baby then, when sat up on the parent's leg,
could smile,
then could recognize the mother,
and then the father,
then could cry like a little chickadee,
and then could babble like a little sparrow.

Now the baby could crawl and play,
and then could walk unsteadily,
and gradually could play with dirt;
day by day the baby grew up,

像竹子一节一节升高，
背着鸭笼会到寨脚放鸭子了，
别着镰刀会上山放牛了，
唱着山歌会挖田了。

众人：萨——萨！

like the bamboo rising section by section,

could carry a duck cage and herd the ducks in the back of the village,

then could carry a sickle on the waist and herd the cattle up in the mountains,

and then could sing the folk song while working in the field.

All people sang: Sa—Sa!

九、杜达纳嘎[1]

萨啦阿依——
哈尼人最先在哪个地方？
后来为哪样又要搬迁？
前前后后在哪些地方栽过磨秋桩？
是哪个先祖，
给我们找到了这可爱的家乡？

（一）

萨啦阿依——
在那遥远的地方，
有一条宽阔的大江，
淌着金子一样的水，
闪烁着耀眼的金光。
江畔有块宽宽的平地，
是个美丽富饶的地方，
这块土地，
是哈尼阿甫②最先生活的家乡。

① 杜达纳嘎：先祖迁徙歌。
② 阿甫：先祖。

IX. Dudanaga①

Sala'ayi—
Where did the first group of Hani people live?
Why did they migrate later?
Where were all the Moqiu stakes built over those years?
Which ancestor
found this lovely home for us?

(I)

Sala'ayi—
In a remote place
was a wide river,
with water flowing like gold,
whose glittering golden reflections were dazzling to the eye.
The wide flat land by the river
was beautiful and fertile.
This land,
was the first home of the Hani Afu②.

---

① Dudanaga: the song of ancestors' migration.
② Afu: ancestors.

最古的时候，
哈尼祖先没有住的地方，
像猴子一样到处跑，
一天在一个地方。
不知过了多少年，
不知换了多少代，
哈尼的祖先，
养起了猪鸡牛羊，
吆着猪鸡到处走，
吆着牛羊到处放。

哈尼吆着猪和鸡，
吆着成群的牛羊，
来到诺玛阿美①。
诺玛阿美是个好地方，
哈尼先祖看上了，
哈尼先祖喜欢了。
砍来直直的木头作柱子，
砍来长长的木头作大梁，
割来茅草和藤子，
盖起了新新的草房；
一边住人堆谷子，
一边关猪养牛羊。

① 诺玛阿美：古地名，在今四川省西昌市一带。

In the oldest days,
the Hani ancestors did not settle in one place
so they ran around like monkeys,
staying in a new place each day.
No one knows how many years had passed,
and how many generations had it been,
before the Hani ancestors
began to raise livestock,
yelling at pigs and chicken all around,
and herding cattle and goats everywhere.

Yelling at their pigs and chickens,
and at their cattle and goats,
the Hani came to Nuoma'amei①.
It was a good place,
which the Hani ancestors were fond of
and which the Hani ancestors chose.
They gathered straight wood as pillars,
long wood as beams,
as well as thatches and rattan,
to build brand new thatched cottages,
one part of which was for people to live and to store grains
and the other part, to raise pigs, cattle and goats.

① Nuoma'amei: name of an ancient place, in about today's Xichang, Sichuan.

选寨头的大树做普玛①，
选寨边的毛木树做竜主②，
选寨脚的草坪作磨秋场。
杀猪祭普玛，
杀狗鸡祭竜主，
杀牛祭磨秋桩；
求天神和地神，
压邪除魔排灾难，
保佑全寨人平安，
保障庄稼无灾害，
保佑六畜肥又壮。

淌着金水的江畔，
美丽富饶的诺玛阿美，
庄稼长得好，
煮出来的米饭特别香；
人养的猪鸡，
多得像山上的雀鸟一样；
人养的牛羊，
多得像搬家的蚂蚁一样。
金色的水，
把世代的哈尼人哺养：
喝金水长大的小伙子，
个个是英俊勇敢的好汉；

① 普玛：护寨神。
② 竜主：压邪除魔树。

They chose the big tree in front of the village as the Puma①,
the woody tree around the village as the Longzhu②,
and the grass field behind the village as Moqiu playground.
They killed pigs to sacrifice to the Puma,
dogs and chickens, to the Longzhu,
and cattle, to the Moqiu stakes.
They prayed to the gods of heaven and earth
to control the evil, to remove the wicked and to expel the disastrous,
to keep all villagers safe and sound,
to protect all the crops from disaster,
and to keep all livestock fat and strong.

By the river where the golden water flowed,
on the beautiful and fertile Nuoma'amei,
the crops grew well,
yielding rice particularly nice.
Pigs and chickens raised by people
were as many as the birds in the mountains.
The cattle and goats tended by the people
were as many as the moving ants.
The golden water
nurtured the Hani people generation after generation:
The young men who grew up on the water
were all handsome and brave;

---

① Puma: guardian of the village.

② Longzhu: the tree for controlling the evil and removing the wicked.

喝金水长大的女儿，
个个是聪明美丽的姑娘。

富饶美丽的诺玛阿美，
哈尼人好吃好住的地方。
每一寸土地，
浸透着哈尼人的血和汗，
每一棵草木是哈尼先祖的命根子，
这里是哈尼先祖安居乐业的天堂。

熟透的甜果子，
容易招来馋嘴的雀鸟；
肥壮的牛羊，
会招来凶恶的豺狼；
美丽富饶的诺玛阿美，
招来了恶人的魔掌。
虎豹一样凶恶的恶人来了，
灾难降到哈尼的头上。

恶人骑着大马，
手里的长刀闪着寒光，
身上披着弓箭，
恶狠狠地闯进哈尼人的家乡。
才发出来的嫩苗，
经不住寒霜摧残；
刚发起来的哈尼人，
难把闯进家乡的恶人抵挡。

the young woman who grew up on the water
were all smart and beautiful.

The beautiful and fertile Nuoma'amei
provided the Hani people with good food and a place to live.
Every inch of the land
contained the blood and sweat of the Hani people,
and every blade of grass was the lifeblood of the Hani ancestors.
Nuoma'amei was the paradise where the Hani ancestors lived and worked in peace.

The ripe and sweet fruits
are likely to attract the sweets-loving birds;
fat and strong cattle and goats,
are likely to court ferocious wolves;
and the beautiful and fertile Nuoma'amei
fell into the clutches of the wicked.
Invaders as vicious as tigers and leopards came,
and disaster befell the Hani people.

The vicious invaders came riding on big horses,
held long knives shining with the chilling light.
carried bows and arrows on their backs,
and savagely broke into the village of the Hani people.
As tender seedlings
could not withstand the cold and frost,
the Hani people that just settled and began to grow
could hardly defeat the brutal invaders of their home.

哈尼人的鲜血，
像河水一样流淌；
哈尼人的头颅，
像石头一样落在地上。
恶人抢走金黄黄的谷子，
赶走了成群的牛羊。
美丽的家园被践踏了，
无辜的哈尼人遭了祸殃。
亲亲的父老兄妹，
恶人霸占了我们的家乡；
我们吃住都不安宁了，
不能再忍受这样的灾难，
赶快背上东西，
赶着成群的牛羊，
牵扶年迈的老人，
背上年幼的儿子姑娘；
大家一起走吧，
去找安居乐业的地方。

众人：萨——萨！

(二)

萨啦阿依——
不知走了多少个白天，
不知过了多少个黑夜，
来到了一座高高的山上，
疲倦的人们停下来休息。
山脚下有个大海，

The blood of the Hani people,
flowed like a river;
the skulls of the Hani people,
fell to the ground like stones.
The wicked invaders took the golden grains
and herds of cattle and sheep.
The beautiful hometown was destroyed,
and the innocent Hani people suffered a catastrophe.
Dear fellow villagers,
the evil invaders occupied our hometown,
where we could no longer eat or live peacefully.
We shouldn't endure this disaster here,
so quickly get all your belongings,
gather your herds of cattle and goats,
assist the elderlies,
bring along the young children on your back.
Together, let's leave this place
to find another place to settle down.

Everyone: Sa—Sa!

(II)

Sala'ayi—
No one knows how many days they had walked
and how many nights they had spent
before they reached a high mountain
and stopped to rest, exhausted.
At the foot of the mountain was a big sea,

海边有个宽宽的坎子；
男女老少看见了，
心里有说不出的高兴。

亲亲的父老兄妹，
我们找到了一块好土地，
这里叫烘阿①，
是个宽宽的坝子，
地平草嫩好养牛羊，
水好土肥好栽谷子；
大家停下来吧，
我们就在这里安寨子。

砍来了长长的大梁，
砍来了粗粗的柱子；
割来了黄黄的茅草，
扯来了牢牢的藤子；
筑起了厚厚的泥墙，
盖起了新新的房子。

普玛安起来了，
竜主建起来了，
磨秋桩也立起来了，
水井挖好了，
哈尼又安起了寨子；

① 烘阿：古地名，据传指今天的昆明。

and by the sea was a broad flat land.
The men and women, old and new, on seeing this,
were unspeakably happy.

Dear fellow villagers,
we just found a good piece of land
named Hong'e①,
a broad riverbank,
where the flat ground and tender grass could feed cattle and goats,
and the clean water and fertile soil could grow crops.
Let's just stop here
to build our village.

Long beams were made out of the lumber gathered,
and so were the thick pillars.
Yellow thatches were collected,
and so were the firm rattan.
The thick mud walls were built,
and then the new houses were completed.

After the Puma was set up,
the Longzhu was installed,
the Moqiu stakes were erected,
and the digging of the well was completed,
the Hani people now built a village once again.

---

① Hong'e: name of an ancient place, said to be today's Kunming.

赶起了热闹的街场，
男女老少欢欢喜喜。
美丽的烘阿，
成了哈尼人生活的土地。

富饶的烘阿，
哈尼生活的地方，
头人管得好，
整个地方平平安安；
贝玛背得好，
百姓没有灾和难；
工匠肯出力，
寨子越来越繁荣兴旺。

幸福的日子，
刚刚滋润了枯朽的心肠，
天大的灾难，
又降到哈尼人的头上：
恶人挥舞着长刀，
又闯到哈尼人的家乡；
受苦的哈尼人，
又遭到了恶人的摧残。

头人当不成官了，
地方乱得像火烧蜂窝；
贝玛背不成了，
百姓多灾多难；
工匠做不成活计，

They organized the busy street fairs,
and men and women, old and young enjoyed themselves.
The beautiful Hong'e,
became the land where the Hani people lived.

The fertile Hong'e,
where the Hani people lived,
was well managed by the headman
and thus safe and sound;
the Beima did a good job praying,
so people were kept away from disasters or trouble;
the craftsmen were willing to work hard,
so the village was more and more prosperous.

The happy days
just helped their withered heart to revive,
when a great disaster,
befell the Hani people again:
the evil invaders, wielding their swords,
broke into the Hani's hometown again;
Poor Hani people,
ravaged again by the evil intruders.

The headman couldn't lead anymore,
and the village was as chaotic as a burning wasp nest;
the Beima couldn't recite and pray any more,
and people suffered disaster and trouble;
the craftsman could not work anymore,

寨子变成一片荒凉。
可怜的哈尼人，
再也无法住在烘阿这地方。

亲亲的父老兄妹，
恶人又闯到我们的家乡，
头人、贝玛和工匠，
受到恶人的摧残；
无辜的百姓，
受尽了天大的灾难。

赶快背上东西，
赶快赶着成群的牛羊，
牵扶年迈的老人，
背上年幼的儿子姑娘，
大家一起走吧，
去找个安居乐业的地方。

不知过了多少条江，
不知过了多少条河，
不知翻了多少座山，
受苦的哈尼人哟，
来到了窝你①这地方。
窝你坝子，
土地肥得像猪板油一样，
草有竹子粗，
高高的杨柳树齐天长。

---

① 窝你：古地名，今开远县。

and the village became desolate.
Poor Hani people,
they could no longer live in Hong'e.

Dear fellow villagers,
the wicked invaded our hometown again,
the headman, Beima and craftsman,
were severely abused;
the innocent villagers,
suffered a great disaster.

Let's quickly carry our belongings,
tend herds of cattle and goats,
help the elderlies,
and carry the young children.
Let's leave together
to find a good place to settle down.

No one knows how many rivers
and streams they had crossed
and how many mountains they had climbed over,
before the poor Hani people
arrived at Woni①.
In that Woni plain,
the soil was as rich as lard,
the grass was as thick as bamboo,
and the tall willow trees grew up to the sky.

① Woni: name of an ancient place, in today's Kaiyuan county.

亲亲的父老兄妹，
我们来到了窝你这地方。
窝你地平水又好，
是块黑油油的肥土地，
水好土肥好栽谷子，
草旺地宽好养牛羊。
大家停下来吧，
我们就在这里盖新房。

肥沃的窝你，
成了哈尼人的家乡，
栽一把秧能收一背谷子，
田棚成了满满的谷仓；
半背谷子能踩一斗米，
煮出来的米饭满坝子香。

人栽的棉花有大树高，
结出的棉桃大得像顶草帽；
满坝盛开的棉花，
像冬天的云海一样；
轧出的棉絮绒又绒，
纺出的棉线细又长，
织出的布匹洁白柔软，
哈尼人穿上了暖和的衣裳。

Dear fellow villagers,
we have come to this place Woni.
The land here is flat and the water, high-quality,
with very fertile and dark soil;
the nourishing water and fertile soil are good for crops,
and the abundant grass in the broad land is good for cattle and goats.
Let's stop here
to build our new houses.

The fertile Woni,
became the home of Hani people,
where a handful of seeds could yield a back-basketful of unhusked rice
and the field sheds became barns filled up with grains.
Half of a back-basketful of unhusked rice could produce ten liters of rice,
and the fragrance of the cooked rice wafted across the riverbank.

The cotton planted was as tall as trees,
with the cotton bolls as big as straw hats;
The cotton plants bloomed all over the riverbank,
like a sea of clouds in the winter.
The rolled-out cotton-wool was velvety,
the spun cotton-thread was thin and long,
and the woven cloth was white and soft:
they gave the Hani people warm clothes to wear.

泥鳅虽然香肥身子短，
幸福的日子过不长；
可怜的哈尼人，
又遭到了天大的祸殃：
七天七夜下大雨，
窝你坝子变成了汪洋；
洪水淹没了庄稼，
洪水冲毁了新房。
没吃没穿熬日子，
男女老少受尽了饥寒。

亲亲的父老兄妹，
老天给我们带来了灾难：
棉树变成了烂草，
谷子陷进了泥塘。
住在窝你，
大家都没心肠，
大家一起走吧，
去找个安居乐业的地方。

牵扶年迈的老人，
背上年幼的儿子姑娘，
苦命的哈尼人，
爬上坝子后面的大山。
男女老少不停歇，
一直追赶落去的太阳。

Just as loaches that are appetizing but small,
the happy days did not last.
Poor Hani people,
suffered a great disaster again:
The heavy rain poured seven days and nights,
turning Woni into a sea;
Their crops were flooded,
so were their new houses.
With no food and no clothes,
men and women, old and young suffered from hunger and cold.

Dear fellow villagers,
heaven brought us this disaster:
the cotton plants became rotten grass,
and unhusked rice sank into the mire.
Living in Woni,
is no longer what we want.
Let's leave together
to find a new place to settle down.

Helping the elderlies,
carrying the young on the backs,
poor Hani people
climbed up the mountain behind the plain.
Men and women, old and young, without any break,
chased the setting sun.

来到了一个宽阔的坝子，
人们都叫它勒昂①。
到处长着黄饭花树，
满坝飘着扑鼻的花香。
恶心的臭气报凶恶，
醉人的花香报吉祥，
男女老少，
都说勒昂是安居乐业的好地方。

男女老少齐动手，
在坝子中间盖起了新房；
宽阔的勒昂坝子，
成了哈尼人的家乡。
一块块地开出来了，
撒上了玉米和高粱；
一丘丘田开出来了，
栽上了绿茵茵的谷秧。

勒昂坝子，
是个好地方，
人栽的庄稼得丰收，
猪鸡鹅鸭多得像蚂蚁，
坝子里到处是肥壮的牛羊；
哈尼吃鱼像吃豆腐渣，
香脆的牛干巴挂满房梁。

① 勒昂：古地名，今建水县。

They came to a broad plain
called Le'ang① by people.
Where the butterflybush flower grew everywhere
with its fragrance filled the riverbank.
Stench signals bad omen,
while intoxicating fragrance of flowers, good luck,
so men and women, old and young,
all said that Le'ang was a good place to settle down.

They all worked together
and built new houses in the middle of the riverbank;
The broad Le'ang bank,
became the home of the Hani people.
Pieces of land were tilled,
and then the corn and sorghum seeds were sowed;
the rice paddy was made,
and then the green rice seedlings were planted.

The Le'ang plain,
was a good place,
where the crops planted were fruitful,
pigs, chicken, geese and ducks became as many as ants,
fat cattle and sheep roamed everywhere on the riverbank,
the Hani people ate fish as often as they ate beancurd dregs
and crispy beefjerkies were hanging all over the beams.

① Le'ang: name of an ancient place, today's Jianshui county.

头人管得好，
整个地方平平安安；
贝玛勤祭献，
百姓没有灾和难；
工匠肯出力，
寨子越来越繁荣兴旺。
哈尼人的儿孙，
一年比一年发展，
人多勒昂坝子住不下，
哈尼要到新的地方辟地盘。

亲亲的父老兄妹，
我们的儿孙一天天发展。
再这样下去，
勒昂坝子会变成街场；
为了子孙后代，
我们去别处辟地盘；
大家分头走吧，
各自去找自己的地盘。

勒昂坝子的哈尼人，
分成十二路去辟地盘：
莫作带人朝东边走四路，
去找安居的地方；
依区带人朝南边走四路，
去找乐业的地方；
仰者带人朝西边走四路，
去找幸福的地方；

The headman managed well,
so the whole area was safe and sound;
The Beima offered sacrificial gifts often,
so the people didn't have disasters or troubles:
The craftsman was industrious,
so the village became more and more prosperous.
The Hani offsprings
became more and more over the years,
and the Le'ang plain became too small for them all,
so the Hani people needed to explore for new settlements.

Dear fellow villagers
we have more children and grandchildren day by day,
If it goes on like this,
the Le'ang plain would be crowded like the street fairs;
For our future generations,
let's go and explore for new settlement places.
Let's go our separate ways
to seek for our own place.

The Hani people in the Le'ang plain
were divided into twelve groups for opening up new areas:
Mozuo led four groups of people to the east
to find places of settlement;
Yiqu led four groups of people to the south
to find places of livelihood;
Yangzhe led four groups of people to the west
to find places of happiness;

还有一部分哈尼，
仍然留下来守勒昂。
众人：萨——萨！

（三）

萨啦阿依——
有本事的仰者，
我们的叶车祖先，
带着父老兄妹，
最后离开勒昂家园，
沿着西边的高山，
一步不停地走向前。

不知爬过了多少座山，
不知经历了多少艰难险阻，
勇敢的哈尼，
来到一座高高的山巅，
看见山南有个宽宽的坝子，
像个木盆放在群山中间。

亲亲的父老兄妹，
平平的坝子就在眼前，
我们就到坝子里安家，
我们就在坝子里栽秧，
世世代代，
就在坝子里过幸福的太平年。

男女老少，

some of the Hani people
stayed to keep developing Le'ang.
Everyone: Sa—Sa!

(III)

Sala'ayi—
the able Yangzhe,
ancestor of the Yeche-Hani,
led some fellow villagers,
left their hometown in Le'ang eventually,
and headed along the high mountain in the west,
marching without any break.

No one knows how many mountains they had climbed,
and how many difficulties they had ventured,
before the brave Hani people
came to a high mountain top,
where they saw a broad plain to the south of the mountain
like a wooden basin placed in the middle of mountains.

Dear fellow villagers,
the flat land is in front of us,
so let's settle down here,
plant the crops here,
generation after generation,
to live here happily and peacefully.

Men and women, old and young,

来到波浪滔滔的元江边，
水深湍急无法过，
望着平平的坝子急得打转转。
聪明的仰者有主意，
用芭蕉树扎成筏子放在水中间，
男女老少，
坐着筏子渡过了天险。

这个坝子叫腊萨①，
夹在两条河中间。
我们的祖先在此安了寨子，
开出了一丘丘良田；
栽出的谷子老实好，
栽出的甘蔗老实甜。
有年腊萨发大水，
洪水愤怒地呼吼，
河边的芦苇被冲走，
粗粗的芦根冲到了河下边。
住在河下游的异族人，
见到芦根烟筒般粗圆，
知道河头有块肥土地，
他们乐得笑眯了双眼。

① 腊萨：古地名，今元江哈尼族彝族傣族自治县。

came by the surging Yuanjiang river,
but the water was too deep and turbulent for them to cross.
Stumped, they could but look at the land from across the river.
The smart Yangzhe came up with the idea
of building the rafts made of banana trees,
and they sent the men and women, old and young,
on the raft across the dangerous river.

This riverbank, named Lasa①,
was flanked by two rivers.
Our ancestors built villages there,
cultivated fertile rice paddies,
grew crops with very good harvests,
and grew sugarcanes that tasted really sweet.
One year there was a flood in Lasa,
the floodwater roaring angrily,
washing away the reeds by the rivers,
and the thick reed roots were rushed down the rivers.
Some non-Hani people who lived downstream,
seeing the reed roots as thick and round as the smoking pipes,
knew the land upstream was fertile
and smiled such a big smile that their eyes could hardly stay open.

---

① Lasa: name of an ancient place, today's Yuanjiang Hani, Yi and Dai Autonomous County.

洪水退去后，
一伙异族人顺河来到腊萨坝，
他们像一群苍蝇碰到了蜜，
借口来打鱼，
久久赖着不肯把家还，
不分白天黑夜，
一下不停地在坝子里头转。

哈尼人安居乐业，
异族人也想沾点光；
数不尽的人跑来寨子，
要求上门做姑爷的话比蜜甜。
先祖仰者心肠软，
招下十个姑爷帮栽田。

十个姑爷非常勤劳，
一年到头不闲一天。
十个姑爷来相伴，
十个姑娘干活日日跑在先。
男女老少，
个个干活不愿闲。
人勤庄稼好，
丰收一年接一年，
有吃有穿人兴旺，
男女老少乐无边。

After the water receded,
a group of those non-Hani people came along the river to the Lasa plain.
Like a horde of flies seeing honey,
they used the excuse of going fishing
to stay here and refuse to leave,
and day or night
they constantly walked around on the plain.

Seeing that the Hani people lived a good life,
those non-Hani people wanted some of their wealth.
Many came to the village,
and those who asked to be Yangzhe's live-in sons-in-law spoke words sweeter than honey.
Yangzhe was soft-hearted
and kept ten of them to help plant the crops.

The ten sons-in-law were so hardworking
that they worked all year round without one day off.
With the companionship of the ten sons-in-law,
the ten daughters worked hard every day.
Men and women, old and young,
all were industrious.
Because of their hard work the crops grew well,
and they had good harvests year after year.
With good food, plenty of clothes, and prosperity,
everyone was very joyful and content.

幸福日子没过多少年，
不幸的灾难驱赶哈尼人搬迁。
十个姑娘，
听信了十个姑爷的蜜语甜言，
叫来他们的公婆，
带着异族的人到门前，
提出要分家，
要分财产和良田。
先祖仰者不答应，
她们又哭又闹咒祖先；
十个狠心的姑娘，
像把长刀戳在先祖的心间。

先祖仰者，
看出姑爷姑娘心里藏着奸，
心想分就分，
趁早割断祸水根源。
他把十对姑娘和姑爷，
一起叫到了面前说：
“姑爷和姑娘，
说说咋个分良田？”

狠毒狡猾的姑爷，
不等姑娘张口先开言：
“亲亲的阿爸，

But happy years didn't last long,

and unfortunately a disaster drove Hani people to move again.

The ten daughters,

duped by the nice words of the ten sons-in-law,

helped to have their father-in-law and mothers-in-law

come to the front doors of the Hani people.

They asked to separate from their parents

and demanded to own their own property and fertile farmland.

When ancestor Yangzhe refused,

the daughters made a scene and wished ill on the ancestor;

the ten cruel-hearted daughters

were like a long knife that broke Yangzhe's heart.

The ancestor Yangzhe

saw through the plot of his daughters and sons-in-law,

and he decided to let them go

so as to sever from the roots of the disaster as early as possible.

He called all the ten young couples

to come and said:

"My sons-in-law and my daughters,

how would you like to divide the farmland?"

The cruel and sly sons-in-law

spoke before the daughters opened their mouths:

"Dear father-in-law,

我们只要一点点，
省得人去熬苦累。
叫只狗来踩田分，
让它走一圈，
圈内就是我们的田。”
先祖仰者不知是毒计，
满口答应让狗踩田分。

十个姑爷叫来一只白狗，
狗尾拴上蘸了油的破布片；
破布片点着火，
吓得白狗叫着绕田坝窜了一圈。
全部良田都被姑爷分走了，
上当的先祖仰者有苦难言。

全部好田被抢走，
哈尼人只好种剩下的一点瘦田。
异族人的心还不满足，
故意把牛放到哈尼人的田中间；
哈尼人的田埂被踩坏，
哈尼人的谷子被践踏。
愤怒的先祖仰者，
砍断一条牛腿丢田边。

we just want a little,
so that we will not be so tired.
How about we call a dog to walk on the field?
Let it walk one round,
and inside the round the land will be ours."
Ancestor Yangzhe didn't know it was a vicious scam
and agreed to use the dog to divide the land.

The ten sons-in-law called out a white dog,
and tied to its tail a rag soaked with oil;
they then set the rag on fire
to scare the dog who then barked and ran around the entire land.
All the fertile land belonged to the sons-in-law,
and the duped ancestor Yangzhe could but accept the result silently.

Having been robbed of all the fertile land,
the Hani people were left with only a little poor field.
But the non-Hani people were still not satisfied
and deliberately let their cattle graze in the Hani people's field;
the ridges of their field were trampled,
and the crops were trodden.
The angry ancestor Yangzhe
cut a leg off the cattle and threw it away by the field.

狡猾的异族人，
来到先祖仰者的身边，
装着低头来认罪，
认错的话说了一遍又一遍：
“豹子抬剩的烂牛，
糟蹋了好好的一片田，
像这样谁见着都会气愤；
砍断牛腿合大家心愿，
往后要是哪家牛来踩，
要比这回处罚更严。”

毒蛇藏在绿草中，
笑脸掩盖着内心的阴险。
我们的先祖仰者，
有天带着猎狗到山上转，
回来的时候，
走过异族人抢占的那片地。
狠毒的异族人，
很快把仰者围在中间：
“上次牛踩田，
你砍了牛腿丢在田边。
牛是不懂道理的，
我们没有说一句怨言；
你是懂道理的人，
故意踩田毁我们的脸面，
今天要砍你的腿，
丢到远远的坝子边。”

The roguish non-Hani people
came to ancestor Yangzhe,
pretending to admit their mistake
and apologizing over and over again,
"the cattle spared by leopards
ruined such a good field,
whoever saw this would be angry;
cutting off its leg is right in everyone's eye,
so from now on if any cattle treads on the field,
the punishment should be even more severe than this."

Poisonous snakes hide in green grass,
and smiling face hides treacherous hearts.
One day our ancestor Yangzhe
took a walk in the mountain with a hunting dog.
On his way back,
he walked through the land embezzled by the non-Hani people.
The vicious non-Hani people
quickly surrounded Yangzhe and said:
"Last time the cattle trampled your field,
you cut off its leg and left it by the field.
The cattle didn't understand,
and till we didn't complain.
But you are a reasonable man,
so you trampled our field on purpose to humiliate us.
Today we will cut off your leg
and threw it far away beyond the riverbank."

异族人举起闪亮的长刀，
哈尼人抬着磨快了的钩镰，
杀声埋葬了歌声，
鲜血染红了富饶的家园。
异族人越打人越多，
哈尼人越斗人越减。

受苦的哈尼人抵挡不住，
退到了腊萨坝子的东边。
我们的先祖仰者，
望着受苦的老少开了言：
“亲亲的父老兄妹，
异族人多势众不怕天和地；
我们哈尼人少势力单，
挨着异族的老牛鞭。
从今以后子子孙孙要代代传：
哈尼人不得招姑爷，
出嫁的姑娘不得分田。

“亲亲的父老兄妹，
仁慈的莫米不睁眼，
哈尼人受尽欺凌，
天神一点也看不见；
十个姑娘是十把长刀，
长刀戳烂了我的心田；
这样下去不得了，
哈尼人的灾难会越来越多。

The non-Hani people raised their shiny long swords,
while the Hani people carried their sharpened hooked spears.
The battle cry drowned out the sound of the songs,
and the blood stained the wealthy homeland.
The longer the fight, the bigger the number of the non-Hani people,
but the smaller the number of the Hani people.

The tormented Hani people could not stop the enemy
and retreated to the east of the Lasa plain.
Our ancestor Yangzhe
looked at the anguish old and young, saying:
"Dear fellow villagers,
the non-Hani people are greater in number and are reckless,
while we are much fewer in numbers and are at an disadvantage,
so we are taking a beat by the non-Hani people.
From now on the lesson should be passed on from generation to generation:
The Hani people would have no live-in sons-in-law,
and daughters married will not be entitled to the family land.

"Dear fellow villagers,
the merciful Momi does not open the eyes,
and so the bullying the Hani people have suffered
the god of heaven sees not at all;
the ten daughters are ten long swords,
piercing through my heart.
If we let this continue, the outcome will be unimaginable,
because the Hani people will suffer even more.

“我们大家走吧，
一个人的心也不要偏，
一个也不要落掉，
一个也不要潜逃；
顺河走下去，
一直走到出太阳的天边边，
为我们的哈尼人，
寻找一个幸福的乐园。

“我们的人多，
只要大家心齐，
毒蛇不敢咬，
魔鬼也不敢挨身边，
老虎不敢来抬吃，
豹子也不敢来舔；
放大胆子快走吧，
乐园就在遥远的前面。”

苦命的哈尼人，
流着悲伤的眼泪，
离开异族霸占的腊萨，
向遥远的东方搬迁。
强壮的男人走前头，
妇女老幼走中间；
拿长刀的男人在前头开路，
防卫的男人手持长矛跟在后边。

白天大家出力赶路程，

"Let's leave here,
be of one heart,
leave no one behind,
and let no one escape;
go along the river,
all the way to where the sun rises.
For our Hani people,
Let's look for a happy paradise.

"We still have quite a few people,
so as long as we are of one heart,
vipers don't dare to bite us,
the wicked don't dare to approach us;
the tigers could not prey on us;
and the leopards dare not lick us;
just walk on boldly,
for the paradise is far ahead."

Poor Hani people,
shedding heartbroken tears,
left the occupied Lasa,
and moved to the east far away.
The strong men walked ahead,
and women, the elderly and the young walked in the middle.
Men with long swords led in the front,
and men with spears brought up the rear.

During the day, they all walked as much as possible,

晚上一群群老虎豹子扑到人跟前。
聪明的仰者主意高，
四周烧起大火防危险；
强壮的男人和猎狗睡边上，
女人和老幼睡中间，
老虎豹子不敢来，
一群群躲进了森林里面。
众人：萨——萨！

（四）

萨啦阿依——
苦命的哈尼人，
我们叶车的老阿波①，
不知过了多少个夜晚，
不知过了多少个白天，
不知爬过多少座山梁，
不知跨过多少条江河，
穿过无边无际的大坝子，
一直顺着元江走到海边。

携带的粮食吃完了，
小娃娃们哭又叫，
年迈的老人累又饿；
我们的祖先仰者，

① 阿波：这里有先祖的意思。

but at night herds of tigers and leopards tried to attack people.
The intelligent Yangzhe had a good idea and
asked people to set the fire in four directions to keep the threat away;
strong men and hunting dogs slept on the outer circle,
while women, the elderly and the young slept in the middle.
The tigers and leopards no longer dared to approach,
and all retreated back into the forest.
All people: Sa—Sa!

(IV)

Sala'ayi—
Poor Hani people
followed the old Abo① of the Yeche-Hani.
No one knows how many nights
and how many days had passed;
no one knows how many mountain ridges they had climbed over
and how many rivers they had crossed.
They went along the endless river bank
of the Yuanjiang River until they came to the seaside.

The food they brought with them was eaten up,
so the young children were crying
and the elderlies were tired and hungry;
our forefather Yangzhe,

① Abo: here it has the connotation of ancestor.

好比针尖戳心窝，
他站在海边上，
一句一句对大家说：
“亲亲的父老兄妹，
幸福的乐园还没有找着，
前面挡着无边的大海，
没有吃的大家都挨饿；
苦命的哈尼人，
又遇到了灾祸。
大家停下来吧，
在这里住上一些日子再说。”

受苦的哈尼人，
在海边平坝上住下来，
男人开田开地种庄稼，
女人拿鱼捞虾采野果。
有水不怕口干，
天气闷热不怕衣裳薄；
没有办法了，
大家只能简简单单过生活。

海边的大坝子，
土地特别肥沃：
棉树要用斧子砍，
谷秆可以做烟筒，

felt like a needle poking his heart.
Standing by the sea,
he said to all pensively:
"Dear fellow villagers,
the happy paradise has not yet been found,
but a boundless sea is blocking our way,
and without food we all are hungry.
Poor Hani people,
will be facing another calamity.
Let's just stop
and stay here for a while and then decide what to do next."

The suffering Hani people,
thus stayed on the flat land by the sea,
men plowing the fields to plant crops
and women fishing for fish and shrimps and picking wild fruits.
With water around, they didn't have to worry about being thirsty,
and in such sultry weather, they didn't have to worry about having but thin clothes.
They had no choice
but to live a very simple life there.

The land by the sea
was quite fertile:
The cotton plants had to be cut with axes;
the rice stalks could be made into smoking pipes;

高粱穗子如马尾，
小米①穗子像雀窝；
哈尼人庄稼丰收了，
收得粮食万千箩。

可怜的哈尼人，
一日两顿饭，
个个肚子饱。
可是天气热得像火烧，
老人小娃热死好几个，
海边的大坝子，
再也没法生活。
祖先仰者说：
“亲亲的父老兄妹，
这里热得住不得，
大人早早就死去，
生下来的小娃不会活。
这样住下去，
我们会死得更多，
我们赶快走吧，
过海去找幸福的乐园谋生活。”

我们的祖先仰者，
肚子里的主意多，
派人找来木头和竹子，

① 小米：这里指一种种植在云南境内的谷科类作物，并非北方的小米。

the sorghum ears were like horse tails;
and the xiaomi① ears were like bird nests.
The Hani people had a big harvest,
reaping thousands of bamboo baskets of grains.

Poor Hani people,
had two meals a day,
and everyone had enough to eat.
But the weather was hot like fire,
the heat killing quite a few elderlies and small children.
The river bank by the sea
was no longer a place to live.
Ancestor Yangzhe said:
"Dear fellow villagers,
in this unbearable heat,
even adults will die young,
and the newborn won't have a chance.
If it goes on like this,
more and more of us will die,
Let's leave without delay
to find a happy place to on the other side of the sea."

Our ancestor Yangzhe
had a lot of ideas.
He sent people to find wood and bamboo

① Xiaomi: a kind of cereal crop planted in Yunnan Province, not the millet in the North.

扎成大大的筏子几十个；
男女老少带上吃的东西，
一个筏子坐一伙，
下海的筏子像筛米，
一直朝出太阳的地方簸。

老天突然扇扇子，
蓝天顿时变成了大黑锅；
无边的大海摇晃起来，
遭了难的哈尼没法逃脱。
刮来一阵大黑风，
连筏带人被海水淹没；
苦难的哈尼人，
又遭到了天大的殃祸。

不知过了多少个白天，
不知熬了多少个黑夜，
可怜的哈尼人，
漂落在海边的沙滩上。
我们的先祖仰者，
被热热的太阳晒活；
他爬起来四处去转，
看看还有多少人活着。

他在沙滩上找了好几天，
好些人还是找不着；
找着的人里头，

to make dozens of large rafts.
Men and women, old and young, took food with them
and got on each raft by groups.
The rafts on the sea bobbed up and down like winnowing rice,
and kept bobbing towards where the sun rose.

As if the sky suddenly flicked its fan,
the blue sky instantly turned into a black wok.
The boundless sea was agitated,
and the trapped Hani people had no way out.
A heavy black wind blew over
and drowned the rafts together with people.
Poor Hani people
suffered another great disaster.

No one knows how many days
and how many nights had passed.
The poor Hani people,
drifted to the beach.
Our ancestor Yangzhe
woke up to the hot sun.
He got up and walked around
to see how many people were still alive.

He searched on the beach for days,
but many people were still not found.
Among those found,

死掉的很多很多，
活着的男女老少只有百十个。
我们的先祖仰者，
带着大家去找地方谋生活。

这里四处是平平的坝子，
到处长满了大树和草根，
没有一座齐天的高山，
没有一条红河样大的江河；
看不到一丝火烟，
看不到一座村落。
哈尼走遍了四面八方，
四面八方都被大海围着。

我们的先祖仰者，
出来的时候对大家说：
“亲亲的父老兄妹，
你们大家都听着，
这个没有人家的地方，
四面八方都被大海围着，
狠心的恶人进不来，
我们不消再遭殃祸；
这是个好地方，
安个幸福的乐园蛮适合。

“太阳从东边出，
慢慢又往西边落；

many, many were dead,

and only more than a hundred of men and women, old and young were alive.

Our ancestor Yangzhe
led them to find a place to make a living.

They came to a large and very flat plains,
where big trees and grass were everywhere,
with no towering mountains,
or a river like Honghe,
or a trace of smoke,
or a village.
They walked all around the place,
only to find that it was surrounded by the sea in all four sides.

Our ancestor Yangzhe
said to everyone when he returned:
"Dear fellow villagers,
listen carefully!
This place where nobody lives
is surrounded by sea in all sides,
so those vicious people could not come in,
and we will not be suffering in their hands again.
This is a good place,
suitable for us to rebuild our home.

"The sun rises from the east,
and sets slowly to the west;

西边淌下来的元江水；
淌到东边的大海里汇合，
大海是水尾，
这地方就叫额咪①啰。
大家定下心来了，
我们就在这里过生活。”

受苦的哈尼人，
在额咪安起寨子，
盖起草房一间间；
寨头建起了普玛一座，
寨边定了一座竜主林，
寨中修了一口井，
寨脚支起一棵磨秋桩；
田地开出来了，
男女老少心里热乎乎。

额咪是个好地方，
平平的土地老实肥沃，
棉树长得一间房子高，
粗粗的谷秆能挂大秤砣；
庄稼年年长得好，
陈谷装满了筐筐箩箩。
额咪家乡年成好，
哈尼人日子过得乐呵呵。

---

① 额咪：天边，水尾。

the Yuanjiang River runs from the west
to join the sea in the east.
The sea is the end of the river,
so let's call this place Emi①.
Let's make up our minds
to settle and make a living here."

Poor Hani people,
settled in Emi.
They built thatched houses one after another,
and the Puma (temple) in front of the village,
marked a part of the bamboo forest by the village as Longzhu forest,
dug a well in the middle of the village
and erected a Moqiu stake at the foot of the village.
After they plowed the fields,
they all felt at home.

Emi was a good place,
where the soil of the flat land was pretty fertile,
the cotton plant grew as tall as a house
and the thick rice stalks could be used as weighing rods.
They had a bumper harvest every year,
with the bamboo baskets filled with rice for years to come.
With a good harvest every year at Emi,
the Hani people lived an enjoyable life.

---

① Emi: the end of the earth, of a river.

额咪这地方虽说庄稼好，
瘴气却像魔鬼一样恶。
瘴气熏得人们头晕眼花，
喝了水后肚子好像胀破；
人着了瘴气发起来，
全身一下发冷一下又发热。
哈尼人来到额咪九年，
年年发瘴气死掉好些人。

我们的先祖仰者，
年年都受瘴气折磨；
杀狗给他打瘴气，
吃了狗肉才得把命活。
瘴气难断根，
隔上一段时间又发作；
虽然人没死，
病得头发已全部掉落。
我们的先祖仰者，
再也忍受不了瘴气的折磨，
他望望西边天，
痛心地对大家说：
“亲亲的父老兄妹，
这里的瘴气老实恶，
这样下去会送掉命，
还是回老家去算啰。”

乡亲们知道故乡好，

Although the crops grew well in Emi,
The jungle fever was devilish.
It made them dizzy and nauseous,
and the water made them so bloated their stomach was to burst open.
Once people became sick with it,
they felt now burning with high fever now chilled to the bone.
During the nine years the Hani people stayed at Emi,
every year quite a few people died of it.

Our ancestor Yangzhe
was tortured by the jungle-fever every year.
People killed dogs to detoxicate his body
and saved his life only by feeding him dog meat.
But it is hard to eradicate the jungle fever,
which kept returning after a while.
Although still alive,
he had lost all his hair.
Our ancestor Yangzhe
could no longer put up with it,
so looking to the sky in the west,
and said to all:
"Dear fellow villagers,
the jungle fever here is really evil,
and we may all lose our lives to it,
so let's return to our hometown."

The villagers knew that their hometown was good,

开始个个都听得心里乐，
可是想到故乡的恶人，
想到过去的灾祸，
想到归途中的风险，
异口同声对仰者说：
“回去九死一生太危险，
还是在额咪过过算啰。”

先祖仰者说：
“大家不走就留下来，
安安心心在额咪生活；
我死也要回故乡，
不然我心里不安乐。”
仰者说完就开路，
坐着筏子离开额咪啰。

众人：萨——萨！

（五）

萨啦阿依——
我们的先祖仰者，
坐着筏子渡大海，
鼓足全身的力气，
拼命直朝西边天划。
老天突然扇扇子，
一阵大风把仰者吹到海边来。
仰者认出自己在元江口，

and were happy to hear this,
but upon thinking of the villains there,
the disasters they had suffered in the past
and the risk they would take on the way home,
they said to Yangzhe in one voice:
"There is little hope we could return alive,
so we may as well stay here in Emi."

The ancestor Yangzhe said:
"You may stay if you don't want to leave
and live a good life in Emi.
But I will go back even if it will cost my life,
for I cannot live my life here."
On saying these words, Yangzhe set off
on a raft and left Emi.

Everyone: Sa—Sa!

(V)

Sala'ayi—
Our ancestor Yangzhe,
was crossing the sea on the raft,
with all his strength,
desperately rowing straight to the west.
Suddenly heaven flicked its fan
and a strong gale blew Yangzhe to a beach.
Yangzhe recognized it was the mouth of the Yuanjiang River
and happily started his journey right away.

高兴得立即把脚迈，
沿着元江一直往上爬，
走得比麂子还要快。
不知过了多少天，
不知过了多少夜，
一个晴天的早晨，
来到腊萨下面的南洼①街。

我们的先祖仰者，
没有自己的家和寨，
没有落脚处，
成了一朵飘游不定的云彩。
有天赶南洼街，
仰者从别处转回来；
在那街场上，
见到岳父慈嘎哥欧乐开怀。
仰者诉说了承受的灾难，
岳父的眼泪挂满两腮。

善良的慈嘎哥欧，
把姑爷领回了自己的山寨，
拿最好的东西给他吃，
找来最好的药给他除病害；
请来最高的贝玛，
把仰者的魂叫回来。

① 南洼：古地名，在今元江哈尼族彝族傣族自治县境内。

He walked up all the way along the Yuanjiang River,
faster than a muntjac.
No one knows how days
and nights he walked,
until a sunny morning
when he came to the Nanwa① street below Lasa.

Our ancestor Yangzhe
did not have his own home or village,
or even a roof over his head,
and wandered alone like a floating cloud.
On the day of the Nanwa fair,
Yangzhe happened to return from his walk.
In the fair,
he happily ran into his father-in-law Ciga Ge'ou.
Yangzhe recounted the disasters he had suffered,
and his father-in-law had tears running down his cheeks.

The kind Ciga Ge'ou,
brought his son-in-law back to his village,
treated him with the best food,
offered the best medicine to cure his disease,
and invited the most able Beima
to call back Yangzhe's soul.

---

① Nanwa: name of an ancient place, in today's Yuanjiang Hani, Yi and Dai Autonomous County.

仰者的魂叫回来了，
仰者的病慢慢好起来，
黑黑的头发长出来了，
疲倦的眼睛闪现了神采。
出门走山路，
比麂子还跑得快。

仰者的老婆在额咪死了，
只是他一个人回来；
差了个老婆，
吃得再好日子也难挨。
我们的先祖仰者，
要讨个老婆自己安寨，
告别善良的岳父，
来到山高林密的江外①。

属马的日子，
仰者来到热闹的马街，
转来转去想找个合心的老婆。
拥挤的街子中间，
红的绿的样样东西都卖，
但是街中间的女人，
没有一张嘴使他感到可爱。

① 江外：元江流域的人们习惯把江的南岸叫“江外”，北岸称“江内”。

When his soul returned,
he recovered slowly.
His black hair grew back again
and his exhausted eyes shone with spirit again.
Walking the mountain path,
he was faster than a muntjac.

Yangzhe's wife had passed away in Emi,
so only he alone came back.
Without a wife,
life was hard even with the best food.
Our ancestor Yangzhe,
wanted to find a wife and build his own village,
so he said goodbye to his kind father-in-law
and came to the high mountains with dense forest in the Outer River Area①.

On the day of the horse,
Yangzhe came to the busy Majie Fair,
and walked around to look for a desirable wife.
The crowded street
was filled with goods of all kinds and all colors,
but none of the women on the middle section of the fair,
was lovely to his eyes.

---

① Outer River Area (Jiangwai): people in the Yuanjiang River region customarily refer to its south riverbank as the Outer River Area and the north of it the Inner River Area.

转来转去地找，
转到街头钻过去钻过来；
热闹的街头，
吃的用的东西样样都有卖，
可惜在街头的女人，
没有一张脸使他喜笑颜开。

转来转去地找，
转到街尾钻过去钻过来；
热闹的街尾，
穿的玩的东西样样都卖，
可惜在街尾的女人，
没有一双眼睛给他带来欢快。

先祖仰者，
赶了马街赶羊街，
跑遍了东西南北，
赶遍了所有的大街小街，
合心的女人，
一个也没有找得来。

先祖仰者，
失望地来到南洼街，
刚走进街子，
一双迷人的眼睛使他发呆：
高耸的胸脯使他高兴，
红润的脸庞使他非常喜爱。
仰者走过去细细一看，
原来是小姨妹欧纽。

He walked and searched
and came to the entrance of the fair.
The busy entrance
was filled with everything to eat and to use,
but sadly none of the women at the entrance
had a face that made him smile and happy.

He walked and searched
and came to the exit of the fair.
The busy exit
was filled with everything to wear and to play,
but sadly none of the women there
had eyes that could bring him joy.

The ancestor Yangzhe,
went from the Majie Fair to the Yangjie Fair,
from the east, to the west, the south, the north,
from big fairs to small ones,
but a woman to his satisfaction,
he found none.

The ancestor Yangzhe,
came back to the Nanwa street disappointed,
But on stepping onto the street,
he was stunned by a pair of charming eyes:
The big bosom delighted him,
and the ruddy cheeks were his favorite.
After Yangzhe walked up to take a closer look
and found it was his sister-in-law Ouniu.

仰者领着小姨妹，
走到岳父慈嘎哥欧的面前，
诉说找不到合心的老婆，
请求再将欧纽嫁给他生后代。
岳父同意了，
仰者领着欧纽到米尼坎①安寨。
不知过了多少年，
不知过了多少载，
我们的先祖仰者，
终于得到了福气，
生了八个儿子，
个个长得老实可爱。

燕子飞去十八回，
门前松树长了十八台，
八个儿子长大了，
仰者将儿子一个个安排：
“我的儿们哟，
请听我把道理说，
我们哈尼人，
经受了数不尽的灾难；
平平的坝子虽然好，
天灾人祸太多我们不能住，
子子孙孙都不要到坝子安寨。

① 米尼坎：古地名，在今红河县境内。

Yangzhe brought his sister-in-law
to the presence of his father-in-law Ciga Ge'ou,
told him that he could not find a satisfactory wife except for Ouniu
and asked him for her hand in marriage to produce children.
The father-in-law agreed,
and Yangzhe took Ouniu to Minikan① to settle down.
No one knows how many years,
and days passed
when our ancestor Yangzhe
was finally blessed
with eight sons,
each of whom very lovely.

After the swallows migrated eighteen times,
and the pine trees in front of the house grew for eighteen years,
the eight sons all grew up,
and Yangzhe gathered them together and said:
"My sons,
please listen to me:
We Hani,
have suffered countless calamities.
Although the flat riverbank is good,
it has too many natural and man-made disasters for us to live here.
Remember never to build villages on riverbanks.

---

① Minikan: name of an ancient place, in today's Honghe county.

"高高的山梁，
山清水秀灾害少；
山高不怕大水淹，
坡陡恶人很难爬上来，
森林茂密难开路，
坏人不敢轻易进山寨；
从今以后，
子子孙孙都在山上安寨。

"亲亲的儿子们哟，
你们要牢牢记在心上，
诺玛阿美是我们的故乡，
宽宽的坝子烘阿是我们的老寨；
窝你、勒昂、腊萨坝子我们住过，
出太阳的额咪有我们的子孙后代，
还有在勒昂分开走了十二路，
东南西北处处有我们哈尼人。
切莫忘记了，
往后有机会要认祖宗互相往来。

"天下的哈尼人哟，
没有先祖就没有我们这一代。
先祖的话做得药，
子子孙孙要牢记在心；

"On the high mountain ridges,

the scenery was green; the water, clean; and disasters, fewer.

In the high mountain we don't have to worry about the flood.

The steep cliffs are hard for the wicked to climb up,

and the dense forests are hard for them to find their way,

so they have to think very carefully before they dare to invade our villages.

From now on,

our offsprings should build villages only in the mountains.

"Dear sons,

bear in mind also

that Nuomaamei was our first hometown

and the broad riverbank Hong'e was our first village;

that Woni, Le'ang and Lasa were where we once lived

and in Emi where sun rises are some of our offsprings;

that twelve groups headed in different directions from Le'ang,

so the Hani people are everywhere.

Remember

to revere our ancestors and to visit each other when you can in the future.

"All the Hani people in the world,

without our ancestors there would not have been us.

Ancestors' words are like medicine,

which should be kept in mind by all the offsprings;

断根的松树要枯死，
忘了祖宗的人活在世上不光彩。
亲亲的父老兄妹，
走到哪里都不要忘记祖宗和后代。”

众人：萨——萨！

just as a rootless pinetree trunk will wither away,

people who forget their ancestors live in disgrace in the world.

My dear villagers,

Let's not forget our ancestors and offsprings wherever we are."

Everyone: Sa—Sa!

十、汪咀达玛[①]

萨啦阿依——
天上的星星，
是太阳月亮生成的；
地上的大树，
是种子长出来的；
世间的男男女女，
是阿爸阿妈生养成的。

爸妈生儿育女，
不像摘移依果一样容易，
不像撒荞子地一样省力；
花费的心血像流水一样多，
使出的力气秤难称。

世间的儿和女，
爸妈的恩情重如山，
要时时刻刻记在心里；
对自己的爸妈，
要尽力服侍孝敬到底。

① 汪咀达玛：孝敬父母。

X. Wangzudama[①]

Sala'ayi —
Stars in the sky
are made possible by the sun and the moon;
trees on the earth
grow up from seeds;
men and women in the world,
are born to and brought up by their parents.

Bearing and rearing sons and daughters
are not as easy as picking wild fruits,
not as effortless as sowing buckwheat seeds in the fields;
it takes care that is as much as the running water,
and stamina that could hardly be weighed by using a scale.

Sons and daughters in the world,
what your parents do for you as great as mountains,
so keep in mind all the time that
for your parents
be respectful and responsible till the very end.

---

① Wangzudama: filial piety.

像小鸡出壳一样，
你一生下地，
呱呱哭着乱滚乱动。

阿爸怕你冷了，
将吃烟的烟筒丢一边，
赶忙拿柴火烧旺火塘；
阿妈怕你冷了，
软软的棉花包了一层又一层，
紧紧抱在怀里让你暖和。
亲亲的阿爸阿妈，
时时把你放在心窝里。

阿爸抱着你喝酒，
香香的酒甜到心窝；
你要撒尿了，
阿爸赶忙放下筷子，
轻轻撑开你的脚。
黄黄的尿撒在地上，
臭气冲进阿爸的喉咙，
亲亲的阿爸不发火，
等你撒完尿照样把酒喝。

阿妈抱着你吃饭，
香香的米饭甜在心窝；
你要屙屎了，
阿妈赶忙搁下饭碗，
轻轻撑开你的小脚。

Like a chick just out of its eggshell,
as soon as you came into this world,
you cried, your arms and legs flailing.

Your papa, worrying that you might be cold,
would put aside his smoke pipe
and hurry to fetch firewood to burn the fire pit.
Your mama, worrying that you might be cold,
would wrap you up with soft cotton layer after layer,
and hold you in her arms tightly to keep you warm.
Your dear papa and mama
would always put you in their hearts.

Your papa would hold you when drinking
and feel the fragrant liquor sweet to his heart;
when you had to pee,
he would quickly put down his chopsticks
and gently opened your legs.
The yellow urine on the ground
scratched his throat with the foul smell,
but he would not get angry,
and go on drinking after you were done.

Your mama would hold you when eating
and feel the fragrant rice sweet to her heart;
when you had to go,
she would quickly put down her bowl
and gently opened your little legs.

黄稀稀的屎沾衣襟，
亲亲的阿妈不动气，
等把你料理干净，
才顾得上把饭碗端起。

你人嫩鼻孔细，
浓浓的鼻涕阻塞换气，
张口咽不下奶水，
换气响得像口熬稀饭的土锅。
阿爸和阿妈，
怕把你嫩嫩的鼻子抠烂，
用嘴含着你的小鼻子，
一口一口把鼻涕吸出。

你人小还不懂事，
见着什么就要什么，
见树上的核桃，
指着要一个；
可是树上的核桃，
青青果皮还没有裂壳。

阿妈为使你欢喜，
连忙支起小土锅，
煮个大鸡蛋，
染上绿色让你吃着。

你见别人吃楼，
嚷着也要吃果果；

Your thin yellow poop stained her clothes
but she would not get angry,
and first clean you up.
before returning to her meal.

When you were little, your nose was small and delicate,
and the thick mucus would block your breathing;
you could not swallow the milk
and you breathing sounded like a pot of porridge boiling.
Your papa and mama,
worried that their fingers might hurt your tender nose,
would use their mouths
to suck the mucus out for you.

When you were little,
you would ask for whatever you saw.
Seeing the walnuts on the tree,
you pointed to them and asked for one,
even though the walnuts on the tree
were still green and uncracked.

To make you happy,
your mama would quickly set up a small earthen pot,
boil a big egg,
and dye it green for you to eat.

When you saw others eating wild fruits,
you also cried for them, too.

你吃一半丢一半，
伸着小手要一个又一个。
阿妈为了满足你，
一天上树摘三次移依果。

你见着天上的星星，
嚷着要一颗；
阿爸没法摘给你，
你的眼泪淌成一条小河。
为了不使你失望，
阿爸捉来萤火虫逗你快活。

你见着天上的月亮，
嚷着要一个；
阿妈没法拿给你，
你差点把阿妈的脸撕破。
为了不让你伤心，
阿妈伤透了脑筋，
踩一块雪白的糯米粑粑，
给你抱着尽情玩乐。

你长大了一点，
像只跳上跳下的松鼠。
暖乎乎的春天，
你拖着锄头当马骑，
嘿哧嘿哧骑到门前，
又拖着往寨子边走去。

You ate half, threw away the rest,
and held out your little hands for one after another.
To satisfy you,
she would climb up the tree and pick them for you three times a day.

When seeing the stars in the sky,
you cried for one.
Your papa could not pick one for you,
and your tears streamed down your cheeks.
In order not to disappoint you,
your papa would catch fireflies to make you happy.

When seeing the moon in the sky,
you wanted it.
Your mama could not get it for you,
and you almost scratched her face.
In order not to make you sad,
your mama would drain her brains,
make a piece of white glutinous rice cake
for you to hold and play.

When you got a little older,
you were like a squirrel jumping up and down.
In the warm spring,
you took a hoe and rode it like a horse
to the front door, panting along,
and then headed out to the village.

骑马的游戏玩够了，
你把锄头丢在草坪上。

阿爸和阿妈，
要去挖田种地，
找不见锄头，
急得像热锅上的蚂蚁。
阿妈气得流眼泪，
阿爸只好低头向人家借。

火一样热的夏天，
乌云一来就下雨。
你像小鸭子见到水塘，
听到水响就欢喜，
悄悄跑出家门口，
不卷裤脚就跳下泥塘里；
开一条沟引水，
打道埂堵作田学使犁。
你玩饱玩够出水来，
新新的衣裳沾满烂泥。
阿爸一天给你洗三次澡，
阿妈一天给你换三回衣。

瓜果熟了的秋天，
你成了一只树上的猴子，
只要枝头还有梨果

After you had had enough with this horse-riding game
you left the hoe on the lawn.

When it was time for your papa and mama
to go and farm in the fields
and could not find the hoe,
they would worry like the ants on a hot pan.
Your mama would be distressed to tears,
while your papa would have to swallow his pride and borrow from others.

In the fiery-hot summer,
the moment black clouds appeared, it rained.
You were like a duckling seeing a pond,
happy upon hearing the sound of water.
You would sneak out of the house
and jump into the muddy puddle without rolling up your pants,
to open a ditch to guide water,
build field-ridges and learn to plough the land.
When you had had enough and got out of the puddle,
your brand-new clothes were covered with mud.
Your papa bathed you three times a day
and your mama changed your clothes three times a day.

In the fruit-ripening autumn,
you turned into a monkey on the tree;
as long as there were still pears left on the branches,

一天不知道爬树多少次。
新新的衣裳撕得开花，
厚厚的裤子磨出口子。
阿爸一天要到树下叫你两回，
阿妈一天要给你补衣裳三次。

牛马不出圈的冬天，
茫茫寒雾从四方升起。
家里的火塘还未冒烟，
你就偷着上山撵雀逗趣。
太阳都落山了，
饭凉三回又热三回，
不见你的影子在哪里，
阿妈焦得到森林边呼唤，
阿爸急得四处寻找你的足迹。

过年过节的时候，
你嚷着要穿新衣；
家里没有银子钱，
阿爸阿妈想方设法打主意：
天不亮阿妈上山背柴卖，
太阳落山阿爸还在外卖苦力。
一滴血汗一分钱，
你能穿上新衣裳不容易。

it would be hard to count how many times you climbed up the tree.

Your brand-new clothes were torn
and your thick pants, ripped.
Your papa would call you from under the tree twice a day
and your mama would sew your clothes three times a day.

In the home- and stable-staying winter,
the vast cold fog rose in all directions.
Before the fire pit at home was lit,
you had snuck out to the mountain to chase birds.
Even after the sun set,
after the dinner had been cold and heated three times,
you were nowhere in sight.
Your mama was so worried that she went to the forest shouting your name
and your papa was so anxious that he looked around for your footprints.

On holidays,
you cried for new clothes,
but there was no money at home,
so your papa and mama tried to make some:
before dawn your mama would go up the mountains and cut firewood to sell,
and after sunset your papa would still be working hard outside.
Every penny they got was paid with their blood and sweat,
so it was never easy for you to wear new clothes.

五月六月闹饥荒，
家里找不出一粒米，
阿妈愁得泪汪汪，
阿爸焦得满脸成了老树皮。
阿爸阿妈为不让你饿坏，
走遍寨头寨脚把米借。
一丝细雨落干田，
借来一碗米难以充饥。

为了养活你，
阿爸上山挖野菜，
进森林被猛兽毒蛇吓得魂飞，
钻草丛给倒钩刺划破背脊；
挖一背篓野菜，
流的血汗如下一场雨。

阿妈低头出家门，
挨村串寨去讨借，
来到寨头被恶狗咬，
下到寨脚受恶人欺；
伸手讨饭抖碎了心，
讨一碗饭流一脸泪。

In May and June before the new grains had arrived,
not one grain of rice could be found at home.
Your mama would be worried to tears,
and your papa, with wrinkles like the bark of an old tree.
To keep you as healthy as possible,
your parents would go over the village to borrow rice.
But like a drizzle fell into the dry field,
a bowl of rice borrowed was far from enough to allay the hunger.

To provide for you,
your papa would go up the mountains to dig for wild vegetables,
even though he was scared to death by the beasts and snakes in the forest
and was cut on his back by the thorns in the bushy grassland.
For every back-basket of wild vegetables,
he shed as blood and sweat like a rainfall.

Your mama walked out of the house hanging her head low,
begging for food from village to village.
She was bitten by vicious dogs entering a village
and bullied by wicked people leaving it.
Her hand reaching out and her heart broken,
for every bowl of rice she paid with tears covering her face.

阿爸挖来了野菜，
阿妈讨来了饭和米；
野菜阿爸阿妈咽，
米饭一颗一粒留给你。
阿妈饿成了扁豆，
阿爸瘦得像条干鱼。

艰难困苦的日子，
像数不尽的树叶，
能换的东西换完了，
能卖的东西已卖出去；
阿爸和阿妈，
唯独没有舍得卖你。

省吃俭用积谷米，
为的是饥荒年成有饭吃；
阿爸阿妈尽心养育你，
盼你像春笋一样快长，
一节一节长成树。
阿妈的心血操干了，
阿爸的力气使尽了，
你已长成大人，
讨了媳妇当家立业。
像转磨一样轮到你了，
切莫把爸妈的恩情忘记。

Your papa returned with the wild edible plants,
and your mama got back with some rice, cooked and uncooked.
Your papa and mama would eat the wild plants,
leaving every grain of the rice for you.
Your mama became so starved she looked like a string bean,
and your papa, like a dried fish.

Days of difficulties and hardships,
were like the countless leaves.
Whatever could be exchanged was.
and whatever could be sold was, too.
Your papa and mama
only kept you, unwilling to sell.

They were frugal with what they used and ate
so as to have food for rainy days like famine;
your parents did their best to bring you up,
wanting you could grow up quickly like a bamboo shoot,
part by part into a big tree.
Your mama gave you all her heart,
and your papa, all his strength.
You have now grown up,
got married and started your own family and career.
Like a turning mill, it is your turn
not to forget what your parents had done for you.

阿妈的脸上垒起沟埂，
阿爸的头上落了一层银霜。
世上的人哟，
个个都要老一回；
做儿女的人哟，
不要学山雀硬了翅膀不回窝，
要拿出一片诚心来孝敬老人，
让他们日子过得快活。

为了养育你，
阿爸阿妈挣伤了腰杆，
苦损了筋骨。
无论生活有多艰难，
无论活计有多繁忙，
你切莫叫爸妈出家门，
上山下地干活计。

磨损的刀难砍柴，
上了年纪的人牙脱落。
阿爸阿妈吃的要精心做：
饭要煮得泡软，
菜要切细煮烂，
让他们吃得又香又甜。

家里办事情，
先要和阿爸阿妈商量；

The wrinkles on your mama's face are deep,
and the gray on your papa's head is like the silvery fog.
People in the world,
everyone will get old once.
Sons and daughters,
don't be like the chickadees who don't return to their nests when their wings become strong.
Instead, look after your parents well with all your heart
and let them live happily.

In order to bring you up.
your parents hurt their backs,
and wore out their muscles and bones.
No matter how hard your life gets,
and no matter how busy you are,
don't let your parents leave the house
to work up on the mountains or down in the fields.

Like the blunt knife that can hardly cut firewood
the elderlies have lost their teeth.
What your parents eat should be prepared carefully:
The rice should be cooked soft,
and the dishes should be chopped finely as well as cooked tenderly,
so that they could enjoy their meals.

With family matters,
discuss first with your parents;

家里有好吃的东西，
先要给阿爸阿妈尝；
过年过节杀鸡鸭，
嫩肉和肝要给爸妈送上。
阿爸喜欢喝口酒，
家里的酒壶不要空；
母亲喜欢烧火塘取暖，
灶前的柴堆不要空。

阿爸阿妈老来脚手硬，
出出进进不灵便。
不论他们到寨子里串门子，
或是走亲串戚到他乡；
不论他们出门去做客，
或是去看望朋友，
做儿女的要多加留意，
送去接回尽儿女心肠。

阿爸阿妈老来怕风寒，
让他们防寒保暖记在心上。
要趁天气还不冷，
为他们早早缝好过冬的衣裳；
十冬腊月到山寨，
不让阿爸阿妈受寒冻，
儿女要多砍些柴，
白天黑夜把火塘烧旺。

世间的儿女，
这是孝敬爸妈的道理。

having delicious food,
give it first to your parents;
butchering chickens and ducks on holidays,
offer the tender meat and livers to your parents.
Papa is fond of drinking a little,
so don't let the flagon be empty;
mama likes to keep the firepit on for warmth,
so keep the firewood by the firepit in stock.

Old papa and mama are stiff,
and cannot walk out and in easily.
Whether they visit others in their village
or relatives in other villages,
whether they go out to be guests,
or visit friends.
being their children you should take care
to take them there and bring them back.

Old papa and mama don't like the cold weather,
so you should make sure to keep them warm.
Before it gets cold,
have their winter clothes ready;
when deep winter arrives at the village,
keep them from the cold.
As their children, you cut more firewood
to keep the firepit on day and night.

Sons and daughters in the world,
this is why filial piety is important and how to practice it.

道理是人间的种子，
一天也不能让它丢失，
一代一代传下去，
世世代代兴下去。

众人：萨——萨！

The why and the how are like seeds in the world:
they cannot be lost for even a day,
should be passed on from one generation to the next,
blooming and bearing fruit generation after generation.

All people: Sa—Sa!

十一、觉车里祖①

萨啦阿依——
最先建街子的是哪个？
最先赶街子的是哪个？
最先建街子的是觉车，
最先赶街子的是汉人。
最先建起来的街子是哪个？
最热闹的街子是哪个？
最先建起来的是烘阿欧德额里②街，
最热闹的是汉人的斗楚③街。

觉麻三弟兄建起麻密寨，
觉麻在麻密寨安了家；
不赶街子不痛快，
不赶街子不热闹。

觉车离开麻密寨，
到各个地方赶街子。

---

① 里祖：赶街。
② 欧德额里：古地名。
③ 斗楚：古地名，地址不详。

Ⅺ. Jueche Lizu[①]

Sala'ayi—

Who was the first that organized the fair?

Who was the first that went to it?

Jueche was the first person who organized the fair

and it was the Han people who first attended it.

Which fair was organized first?

Which one was the busiest and liveliest?

The first fair was Oude Eli[②] in Hong'e,

and the liveliest one was Douchu[③] of the Han people.

After Juema and his two brothers built the Mami village,

Juema settled down there;

but without going to the fair he was not living to his heart's content

and life did not feel jolly and fun enough to him.

Jueche left the Mami village,

going to different places to find one for the fair.

---

① Lizu: go to fairs.

② Oude Eli: name of an ancient place.

③ Douchu: name of an ancient place, today's location unknown.

觉车来到竜特①这地方，
转来转去眼睛四处瞧：
高高的山顶下，
清清的龙潭旁，
密密的树林中间，
有一块宽宽的平地，
是个赶街的好地方。

觉车跑到各个村寨，
把赶街的事情告诉人们：
“龙日是个吉祥的日子，
竜特这地方要赶龙街。
街上买吃的人老实多，
要卖吃的就去赶龙街；
街上买穿的人老实多，
要卖穿的就去赶龙街；
街上买用的东西老实多，
要卖用的东西就去赶龙街。
街上吃的东西样样有，
要换吃的就去龙街上；
街上穿的东西样样有，
要换穿的就去龙街上；
街上用的东西样样有，
要换用的就去龙街上。”

① 竜特：古地名，今红河县境内的浪堤乡。

He came to Longte①,
walking and looking around:
below the high mountain top,
beside the clear Longtan spring,
and in the middle of the dense forest
there was a broad flat land,
a good place for the fair.

Jueche hurried to each village
telling everyone about the fair:
"The day of dragon is an auspicious day,
and there will be a Longjie fair in Longte.
Many at the fair will want to buy food to eat,
so if you want to sell food, go to the Longjie fair;
many will want to buy clothes to wear,
so if you want to sell clothes, go to the Longjie fair;
many will want to buy tools and wares to use,
so if you want to sell those, go to the Longjie fair;
there will be foods of all kinds there,
so if you want to trade foods, go to the Longjie fair;
there will be all kinds of clothes there,
so if you want to trade clothes, go to the Longjie fair;
there will be all kinds of tools and wares to use there,
so if you want to trade those, go to the Longjie fair;

---

① Longte: name of an ancient place name, today's Langti township in the Honghe County.

到了属龙那一天，
赶街的人像沟水一样淌来：
赶马做生意的汉人来了，
穿宽袖衣裳的傣家妇女来了，
穿短裤的叶车姑娘来了，
戴公鸡帽的彝家姑娘来了，
会打麂子的仆拉汉子来了，
穿短衣裳的罗美老表来了；
各种各样的人都来了，
四面八方的人都来了。

龙街街子老实热闹，
赶街的人像蚂蚁一样多，
赶街人的声音，
像打雷一样响。
街上吃的东西样样有：
通海的黄烟黄生生，
石屏的白鱼亮晶晶，
汉人的冰糖甜又脆，
仆拉的茄子有碓嘴粗，
哈尼的泥鳅黄鳝老实肥；
卷粉凉粉到处摆，
猪肉牛肉满街香……

街上穿的东西样样有：
汉人的丝线刺眼睛，
白布花布俏生生，
彝家的棉花白花花；

On the day of dragon,
fair attenders flowed into the street like water through a canal:
Han businessmen with their horses,
Dai women in their wide-sleeved clothes,
Yeche girls in their shorts,
Yi girls in their cockscomb hats,
Pula hunters of muntjac,
and Luomei cousins in short clothes.
People of different ethnic groups came
from all directions.

The Longjie fair was quite lively,
where people were as many as ants,
and the sound they made
was as loud as thunder.
Food of all kinds were available:
the yellow tobacco of Tonghai,
the shiny whitefish of Shipin,
the sweet and crispy rock sugar by the Han people,
the pestle-thick eggplant by the Pula people,
the fat loach and eels by the Hani people,
steamed rice noodle roll and bean jelly everywhere,
and the aroma of pork and beef all over the street...

Clothes of all kinds were available at the fair:
The shining silk threads of the Han people,
the fine white and colorful cloth,
the white cotton of the Yi people,

银子镯头亮闪闪，
染布的蓝靛青幽幽，
鞋子帽子摆成一排排，
衣裳裤子摆成一层层。

街上用的东西样样有：
锄头斧子砍刀摆地上，
犁耙簸箕和篾簿放地上；
叶车人织的席子滑噜噜，
仆拉人编的背箩铁扎扎；
大小银针一包包，
麻布口袋一打打，
土锅瓦罐堆一片。

街子边边上，
卖的大猪小猪一窝窝，
黄牛水牛骡马一大场，
鸡鸭装在笼子里，
狗像牛角弯弯地躺在地上，
山羊“哞哞”叫，
小猫在鸡笼里抓。

要买的东西买着啰，
要卖的东西卖掉啰；
小伙子瞧着姑娘啰，
小姑娘遇着小伙啰。
赶街大家都好玩，

the shining silver bracelets,
the dark blue indigo for dyeing,
rows and rows of shoes and hats,
and stacks and stacks of clothes and pants.

Tools and wares of all kinds were available at the fair:
Hoes, axes and choppers displayed on the ground,
ploughs, winnowing fans, and bamboo silkworm trays all over the ground;
the glossy mats made by the Yeche people,
the sturdy bamboo back-baskets woven by the Pula people
bags of silver needles in different sizes,
dozens and dozens of sacks,
and piles and piles of potteries.

By the street
were sold litters of pigs and piglets,
flocks of cattle, buffaloes, mules and horses,
cages of chicken and ducks,
horn-shaped dogs lying on the ground,
baa-baa sounding goats
and cooped-up kittens in the chicken cage.

People bought what they wanted to buy
and sold what they wanted to sell;
young men looked at girls
and girls met young men.
Going to the fair was fun for everyone

赶街大家都喜欢，
从此一到属龙的日子，
大家都来赶街啰。

觉车高兴了，
觉车欢喜了，
单赶一个街子太孤单，
还要建更多的街子才热闹。
觉车又到别处转，
去选赶街的地方。

觉车来到叶车这地方，
转来转去到处瞧：
高高的山底下，
宽宽的坎子旁边，
长长的河上面，
一个大大的垭口上，
有一块宽宽的草坪，
是个赶街的好地方。

觉车跑到各个寨子，
把赶街的事情告诉人们：
“羊日是个吉祥的日子，
叶车这地方要赶羊街①啰。
街上的东西老实多，
要买东西就去赶羊街；

① 羊街：地名，在红河县境内。

and was liked by everyone,
so from then on, on the day of dragon,
people all went to the fair.

Jueche was delighted
and happy,
but one fair was not enough,
and it would be lovely if there were more.
So Jueche went to somewhere else
to find a place for the fair.

Jueche came to Yeche,
walking and looking around:
at the foot of the high mountain.
beside the broad embankment,
above the long river,
on a big mountain pass,
an area of wide grassland,
a good place for the fair.

Jueche went to each village,
telling people about the fair:
"The day of goat is an auspicious day,
and there will be a Yangjie fair at Yangjie① in Yeche.
There will be various things at the fair,
so if you want to buy some things, go to the Yangjie fair;

---

① Yangjie street: name of a place, is in the Honghe county.

街上买东西的人老实多，
要卖东西的就去赶羊街；
街上俏俏的姑娘老实多，
要瞧姑娘的就去赶羊街；
街上称称①的伙子老实多，
要瞧伙子的就去赶羊街。”

到了属羊那一天，
赶街的人像搬家的蚂蚁一样走来：
背戥子做生意的汉人来了，
挑竹篮的傣家伙子来了，
会打马鹿的瑶家来了，
戴白布帽的叶车女人来了，
戴银珠帽的彝家姑娘来了，
穿短衣裳的罗美人来了。
各种各样的人都来了，
四面八方的人都来了。

羊街街子老实热闹，
赶街的人有一升芝麻粒多，
街场上的说话声，
像雨天暴发的洪水一样响。

街上吃的东西样样有：
玉溪的烟丝黄生生，
新平的酒药白花花，
磨黑的盐巴一驮驮，
元江的红糖一箩箩；

---

① 称称：标致，漂亮。

many people will want to buy some things at the fair,
so if you want to sell some things, go to the Yangjie fair;
many beautiful girls will be at the fair,
so if you want to see them, go to the Yangjie fair;
Many handsome lads will be at the fair,
so if you want to look at them, go to the Yangjie fair."

On the day of the goat,
fair attenders walked to the fair like ants moving their homes:
Han businessmen with tiny scales,
Dai lads shouldering bamboo baskets,
Yao hunters of red deer,
Yeche women in white cloth hats,
Yi girls in silvery-bead hats,
as well as Luomei people in short clothes.
People of different ethnic groups came
from all directions.

The Yangjie fair was really lively,
with as many people as a liter of sesame,
and their voice on Yangjie street
was as loud as the flood on a rainy day.

Foods of all kinds were available at the fair:
the yellow cut tobacco of Yuxi
the white medicinal liquor of Xinping,
packs of salt from Mohei,
baskets of brown sugar from Yuanjiang,

傣家的荔枝甜蜜蜜，
彝家的花生香噜噜，
哈尼的螺蛳一背背，
仆拉的粗烟一把把，
叶车的谷子黄灿灿，
罗美的大米齐刷刷；
米线卷粉到处摆，
猪肉牛肉炒得满街香。

街上穿的戴的样样有：
白布青布滑噜噜，
银链银镯亮闪闪，
丝线花辫惹人爱，
衣裳裤子摆得一层层，
鞋子帽子摆得一排排。

街上用的东西样样有：
锄头镰刀摆地上，
谷船篾桌置地上，
叶车的蓑衣大又厚，
建水的瓦货排成行，
通海的小刀快又亮；
街子边的草地上，
一大群牛躺在树荫下，
拴在桩桩上的大猪小猪摇尾巴，
鸡鸭一笼笼，
红脚鸽子一对对，
拴着的狗哭叫着咬索子。

sweet lychees from the Dai people,
tasty peanuts from the Yi people,
back-baskets of spiral shells from the Hani people,
bundles of tobacco leaves by the Pula people,
golden-yellow grains by the Yeche people,
plump rice by the Luomei people,
rice noodles and steamed rice noodle rolls everywhere,
and the aroma of stir-fried pork and beef filled the air.

All kinds of clothes and accessories were available at the fair:
Glossy white and black cloth,
sparkling silver necklaces and bracelets,
lovely colorful braids of silk threads,
stacks and stacks of shirts and trousers,
rows and rows of shoes and hats.

All kinds of tools and livestock were available at the fair:
Hoes and sickles laid on the ground
boat-shaped threshers and bamboo tables in display,
big and thick straw rain-capes by the Yeche people,
rows of tiles from Jianshui,
and sharp and bright knives from Tonghai.
On the grassland by the fair,
a herd of cattle lying in the shade of the trees,
pigs and piglets tied on stakes wagging their tails,
cages of chicken and ducks,
pairs of red-foot pigeons,
and chained dogs barking and biting the leash.

需要的东西买着啰，
背来的东西卖掉啰；
小伙子看上了心爱的姑娘啰，
姑娘跟合心的伙子约会啰。
赶街人人都得到好处，
赶街人人都得到欢乐，
从此一到属羊的日子，
大家都来赶羊街。

觉车高兴了，
觉车欢喜了，
可是他还不满足，
还要赶更多的街子。

觉车转到各个地方，
去建新新的街子：
转到车乌①赶牛街，
转到打勐②赶猪街，
转到阿丕③赶马街，
转到保玛④赶鼠街，
转到西竜⑤赶兔街，

① 车乌：地名，在红河县境内。
② 打勐：地名，在元江哈尼族彝族傣族自治县境内。
③ 阿丕：地名，在红河县境内。
④ 保玛：地名，在红河县境内。
⑤ 西竜：地名，在元江哈尼族彝族傣族自治县境内。

People bought what they needed
and sold what they carried on their backs;
lads fell in love with girls of their dreams,
and girls hung out with lads of their expectations.
Every fair-attenders benefited from it
and was joyous,
so from then on, on the day of goat,
everyone went to the Yangjie fair.

Jueche was delighted
and happy,
but he still did not think that was enough
and wanted to make more fairs available,

So he inspected more locations
to organize new street fairs:
he organized the Niujie fair in Chewu①,
the Zhujie fair in Dameng②,
the Majie fair in Api③,
the Shujie fair in Baoma④,
the Tujie fair in Xilong⑤,

---

① Chewu: name of a place, in today's Honghe County.

② Dameng: a place name, in today's Yuanjiang Hani, Yi and Dai Autonomous County.

③ Api: name of a place, in today's Honghe County.

④ Baoma: name of a place, in today's Honghe County.

⑤ Xilong: name of a place, in today's Yuanjiang Hani, Yi and Dai Autonomous County.

转到河坝①赶虎街。
他转遍了各个地方，
十二个日子都赶起街了。

觉车高兴了，
觉车欢喜了，
可是单赶十二个日子的街不如意，
还要赶更多的街子。

觉车来到瓦渣②这地方，
转来转去到处瞧：
高高的山脚下，
宽宽的坝子上边，
清清的龙潭旁，
有一块宽宽的草坪，
是个赶街的好地方。

觉车跑到各个寨子，
把赶街的事情告诉人们：
“老博③是个好地方，
大家快去赶老博街啰。
街上样样东西都有，
要买哪样东西就去赶老博街；
街上好多人等着买东西，

① 河坝：地名，在红河县境内。
② 瓦渣：地名，在红河县境内。
③ 老博：地名，在红河县境内。

and the Hujie fair in Heba①,
He went to all places,
and organized fairs for all the 12 zodiacal days.

Jueche was delighted
and happy,
but even twelve fairs were not enough
and he wanted even more.

Jueche came to Wazha②,
walking and looking around:
at the foot of the high mountains
on the broad plain
by the clear Longtan spring
was an area of wide grassland,
a good place for a fair.

Jueche hurried to every village,
telling people about the fair:
"Laobo③ is a good place,
so go to the Laobo fair.
Things of all kinds will be available at the fair,
so go to the Laobo fair to buy whatever you need;
many will be waiting in lines to buy things,

---

① Heba: name of a place, in today's Honghe County.
② Wazha: name of a place, in today's Honghe County.
③ Laobo: name of a place, in today's Honghe County.

要卖哪样东西就去赶老博街；
街上的姑娘像花一样俏，
要瞧姑娘就去赶老博街；
街上的伙子像金竹一样标致，
要找男人就去赶老博街。"

到了赶街那一天，
赶街的人像回窝的蜜蜂一样飞来：
赶马做生意的汉人来了，
挑竹篮的傣家来了，
戴包头的哈尼姑娘来了，
抬烟锅的彝家伙子来了，
敢打老虎的瑶家汉子来了，
会喝酒的仆拉老倌来了。
各种各样的人都来了，
四面八方的人都来了。

老博街子老实热闹，
赶街人像山上的树一样多，
街场的喧哗声，
像野火烧山一样响。

街上吃的东西样样有：
蒙自的刀烟黄生生，
磨黑的盐巴白花花，
石屏的白鱼亮闪闪，
建水的红糖红生生，

so go to the Laobo fair to sell whatever you want;
girls on the street are beautiful like flowers,
so to see them, go to the Laobo fair;
lads on the street are as perfect as the golden bamboo,
so to find your guy, go to the Laobo fair;"

On the day of the Laobo fair,
people flocked to it like bees returning to their hives:
Han businessmen with their horses
Dai people shouldering their bamboo baskets,
Hani girls in their turbans,
Yi lads with their long smoking-pipes,
Yao young men who dared to fight tigers,
Pula old men who were fond of liquor.
People of different ethnic groups came
from all directions.

The Laobo fair was indeed lively
with people as many as trees in the mountains.
The noise they made at the fair
was as loud as a burning mountain wildfire.

Foods of all kinds were available at the fair:
The yellow cut tobacco from Mengzi,
the white salt from Mohei,
the shining whitefish from Shipin,
the red brown sugar from Jianshui,

伯纳①的荞粑粑香喷喷；
傣家的芒莓②老实甜，
哈尼的谷子满街场，
彝家的紫米紫又亮；
草包鸡蛋鸭蛋一背背，
淌油的火雀一串串，
木耳香菌一箩箩，
刺竹笋子一堆堆，
卷粉凉粉到处摆，
猪肉牛肉满街香。

街上穿的戴的样样有：
白布青布滑噜噜，
银链银镯亮闪闪，
丝线花辮有七色样，
毛巾花布有七十二种花，
衣裳裤子摆得一层层，
鞋子帽子摆得一排排。

街上用的东西样样有：
锄头镰刀一把把，
背箩饭兜一堆堆，
土锅土缸摆地上，

① 伯纳：地名，在红河县境内。
② 芒莓：芒果。

the sweet-smelling buckwheat cakes from Bona①,
the very sweet mangoes by the Dai people,
the grains everywhere on the street by the Hani people,
the purple and bright purple rice by the the Yi people;
back-baskets of eggs and duck-eggs wrapped in muddy straws,
skewers of oily roasted fire-finches,
the bamboo baskets of edible fungus and mushrooms,
piles of spiny-bamboo shoots,
steamed rice noodles roll and bean jelly everywhere,
and the aroma of stir-fried pork and beef all over the street.

Clothes and accessories of all varieties were available at the fair:
Glossy white and black cloth,
sparkling silver necklaces and bracelets,
silk threads and colorful braids in seven colors,
towels and colored-cloths printed with seventy-two kinds of flowers,
stacks and stacks of shirts and pants,
rows and rows of shoes and hats.

Tools and cookware of all varieties were available at the fair:
Hoes and sickles one by one,
piles of bamboo back-baskets and lunch-bags,
clay pots and jars displayed on the ground,

① Bona: name of a place, in today's Honghe County.

碗罐瓦盆随人拣；
倮卜①的篾帽亮闪闪，
左能②的席子滑又亮。

街子边上哟，
卖的牛马一群群，
山羊"哞哞"叫一帮帮，
大猪小猪一大片，
鸡笼鸭笼摆了一大场，
猫在鸡笼里打瞌睡，
狗像牛角弯弯地睡在地上。

要买的东西买着啰，
要卖的东西卖掉啰；
小伙子瞧上姑娘啰，
姑娘瞧着伙子啰。
赶街个个都好玩，
赶街人人都喜欢，
从此一赶老博街，
大家都从四面八方聚拢来。

觉车欢喜啰，
觉车高兴了，
可是他还不满足，
还要赶更多的街子。

---

① 倮卜：地名，在红河县境内。
② 左能：地名，在红河县境内。

ceramic bowls and basins to be picked by everyone;
shiny bamboo hats of Luobo①,
and smooth and glossy mats of Zuoneng.

By the fair
were for sale herds of cattle and horse,
flocks of baa-baa sounding goats,
a crowd of pigs and piglets,
cages of chicken and ducks everywhere,
dozing cats in chicken coops,
and dogs curling like horns snoozing on the ground.

People bought what they wanted to buy,
and sold what they wanted to sell.
Lads took to girls,
and girls took a fancy to lads.
Going to the fair was fun for everyone,
and was what they were delighted to do.
From then on, when it was time for the Laobo fair,
people from all directions gathered there.

Jueche was delighted
and happy,
but he still felt it was not enough
and wanted to organize more fairs.

---

① Luobo: name of a place, in today's Honghe County.

觉车转到各个地方，
去建新新的街子：
转到腊哈①赶新街，
转到多仰②赶牛洪③街，
转到伯纳赶达德④街，
转到洛恐⑤赶戈比⑥街。
转到思陀⑦赶仰书德街，
转到老密⑧赶尼倮街；
虚洛⑨街子赶起来了，
里沙⑩街子赶起来了，
合然街子赶起来了，
布洪街子赶起来了，
勐只街子赶起来了，
依玛街子赶起来了……

觉车转遍了各个地方，
在世间建起了七十二个街子；
七十二个街子七十二个名字，

---

① 腊哈：地名，在红河县境内。
② 多仰：地名，在绿春县境内。
③ 牛洪：地名，在绿春县境内。
④ 达德：地名，在红河县境内。
⑤ 洛恐：地名，在红河县境内。
⑥ 戈比：地名，在红河县境内。
⑦ 思陀：地名，在红河县境内。
⑧ 老密：地名，在红河县境内。
⑨ 虚洛：地名，在红河县境内。
⑩ 里沙：地名，在红河县境内。

Jueche went to different places
to organize new fairs:
the Xinjie fair in Laha①,
the Niuhong② fair in Duoyang③,
the Dade④ fair in Bona,
and the Gebi⑤ fair in Luokong⑥.
The Yangshude fair in Situo⑦ started,
so did the the Niluo fair in Laomi⑧;
the Xuluo⑨ fair started,
so did the Lisha⑩ fair,
the Heran fair,
the Buhong fair,
the Mengzhi fair,
the Yima fair...

Jueche went to all the places,
organized seventy-two fairs in the world
on seventy-two streets and with seventy-two names.

---

① Laha: name of a place, in today's Honghe County.
② Niuhong: names of two places, in today's Lvchun County.
③ Duoyang: names of two places, in today's Lvchun County.
④ Dade: names of places, in today's Honghe County.
⑤ Gebi: names of places, in today's Honghe County.
⑥ Luokong: names of places, in today's Honghe County.
⑦ Situo: names of places, in today's Honghe County.
⑧ Laomi: names of places, in today's Honghe County.
⑨ Xuluo: names of places, in today's Honghe County.
⑩ Lisha: names of places, in today's Honghe County.

各个街子赶起来，
世间一天天热闹起来了。
男女老少都好玩，
四面八方的人都喜欢，
街子一天也不会打失，
人们一天也不会把觉车忘记。

众人：萨——萨！

With all the fairs,
life became more and more interesting.
Men, women, old and young all had fun,
and people in all directions were delighted.
They will not miss any of these fairs,
and they will never forget Jueche.

Everyone: Sa—Sa!

十二、伙及拉及[①]

冬月

萨啦阿依——
旧的一年过去，
新的一年[②]
开始了。
冬月哪样虫虫叫？
草窠里的蛐蛐叫。
河坝的雾气，
像长翅膀一样飞来了；
冷风刮进寨子，
翻动房头上的茅草；
小鸟缩在墙角不动，
树上的落叶满地跑。

冬天不来，
牛马不得养身子；
冬天不来，

① 伙及拉及：一年四季。
② 按哈尼族历法，冬月为一年的岁首。

Ⅻ. Huojilaji[①]

November

Sala'ayi—
An old year had passed,
a new year[②]
had begun.
What insects cried in November?
The crickets in the grass.
The fog from the riverbank
came over as if it had wings;
the cold wind blew into the village,
fluttering the thatches on the roof;
little birds huddled at the corner,
and fallen leaves were blown all over the ground.

If winter did not come,
cattle and horses wouldn't be able to rest;
if winter did not come,

① Huojilaji: the four seasons of the year.

② According to the Hani calendar, the beginning of a year is a winter month.

草木不得睡觉。
勤劳的人，
冬天是备耕的好时节，
不要怕冷风像针戳，
不要怕冰水裂开手脚，
上山砍荞地，
下山开梯田，
挖田打埂要抓紧，
灌满田水心安闲。

众人：萨——萨！

腊月

萨啦阿依——
旧的一月过去了，
新的一月来到。
高山铺冰雪，
寒雾罩寨子；
大树砍得断，
雾帐撕不开；
地上蛇不跑，
天上虫不飞。
虫为什么不飞？
钻进土里去了。
蛇为什么不跑？
缩在洞里睡觉了。

grass and trees wouldn't get to sleep.

For industrious people,

winter was a good time to prepare for ploughing and sowing.

They were not afraid of the cold wind pricking them like needles,

or the icy water cracking their hands and feet.

They went up the mountains to plough buckwheat land

and down to build terraced fields.

They raced with time to plough the fields and make the ridges

and felt at ease when the fields was filled with water.

Everyone: Sa—Sa!

December

Sala'ayi—

An old month had passed,

and a new month had begun.

Mountains were covered with snow and ice,

and the cold fog veiled the village;

Big trees could be cut down,

but the net of the fog couldn't be torn;

Snakes on the ground didn't crawl

and insects in the sky didn't fly.

Why didn't the insects fly?

They had burrowed into the soil.

Why didn't the snakes crawl?

They were sleeping in their holes.

什么树叶枯树不死？
山坡上的麻栗树。
什么树死叶不枯？
山谷里的蕨蕨草。

高山飘雪花，
寨旁的梨树要死一回了，
路边的蒿枝要死一回了，
地上的茅草要死一回了。

草枯根不死，
蛆虫冬睡人不要贪闲，
快离开火塘，
把蓑衣披上，
修好田间的水沟，
积满寨边的粪塘。

众人：萨——萨！

正月

萨啦阿依——
旧的一月过去了，
新的一月来到。
过了一日变一日，
翻过一月是一样，
雾气慢慢散尽，

What tree would not die even with its leaves withered?
It was the chestnut trees on the hillside.
What tree would die but its leaves didn't wither?
The fern in the valley.

When it snowed in the mountains,
the pear trees by the village would be dormant,
so would the wormwood by the road,
and the thatches on the ground.

Leaves fell but the roots were still alive,
so even though maggots hibernated people would not be idle.
They promptly got away from the fire pits,
put on the straw rain-capes
to fix the ditches in the fields,
and fill up the compost pit by the village.

Everyone: Sa—Sa!

January

Sala'ayi—
An old month had passed,
and a new month had begun.
Everyday was different,
so was every month.
The fog gradually dissipated,

竹子尖尖吹笛箫①。
大地醒来了，
大地要翻身了。

小虫从洞里伸出头，
树木冒起芽苞；
四周听见小虫的叫声，
树林里有鸟叫的声音。
河坝里先发芽的是什么树？
河坝里先发芽的是杨柳树。
高山上先冒头的是什么草？
高山上先冒头的是蕨蕨草。

寨边樱桃开花，
沟边索可玛依②飘香，
山顶妥底玛依③怒放，
河坝木棉花染红树梢。

正月来了，
鸟儿飞出来找食：
最先飞来的是燕子，
布谷鸟也跟着飞来了。
燕子从哪里飞来？

---

① 这句的意思是春风吹竹梢，发出响声。
② 索可玛依：七里香花。
③ 妥底玛依：红杜鹃花。

and the tender bamboo shoots were whistling①.
The earth woke up,
so would everything on it, very soon.

Little bugs stuck their heads out from their holes,
as trees budded;
bugs' buzzing was heard all around,
so was birds' chirping in the forests.
Which tree sprouted first on the riverbank?
It was the willow tree that sprouted first on the riverbank.
What grass sprouted first on the high mountains?
It was the fern that sprouted first on the high mountains.

The cherry by the village blossomed,
as the Suokemayi② by the water spread fragrance,
the Tuodimayi③ at the mountaintop was in full bloom,
and the Kapok by the riverbank colored the tree-tips red.

When January came,
birds flew out to look for food:
swallows arrived first,
and were followed by cuckoos.
Where did the swallows fly from?

---

① The sound of wind blowing the bamboo shoots.

② Suokemayi: the evergreen shrub daphne odera.

③ Tuodimayi: the shrub rhododendron simsii.

从遥远的沙咪中仰①飞来，
那里有茫茫的格通大海，
还有九重高的围墙。
布谷从哪里飞来？
从遥远的沙咪中仰飞来，
那里有茫茫的格通大海，
还有九重高的围墙。

格通大海有多宽？
哈南②要飞七天。
格通大海有多长？
鸿回③要飞十个早上。
燕子飞过大海，
布谷飞过大海；
燕子先飞到哈沙④；
布谷跟着飞到哈沙；
一支飞到傣家河坝，
一支飞到汉人住地，
一支飞到哈尼山乡。
一路飞来一路叫：
春天来到了！

燕子飞进山寨，
燕窝筑在屋梁上；

① 沙咪中仰：大海中的岛屿。
② 哈南：乌鸦。
③ 鸿回：斑鸠。
④ 哈沙：元江。

They flew from Shamizhongyang① far away,
where there were boundless Getong Sea
and the high walls reaching the sky.
Where did cuckoos fly from?
They flew from Shamizhongyang far away,
where there were boundless Getong Sea
and the high walls reaching the sky.

How wide was the Getong Sea?
It took Hanan② seven days to fly across it.
How long was the Getong sea?
It took Honghui③ ten mornings to fly along it.
Swallows flew over the sea,
and cuckoos then flew over the sea.
swallows first got to Hasha④.
and then cuckoos got to Hasha;
some flew to the riverbank of the Dai people,
some to the dwelling place of the Han people,
and some to the mountain where the Hani people lived.
They flew, crying all the way:
spring has coming!

The swallows flew into the village,
made their nests under the eaves,

① Shamizhongyang: an island in the sea.
② Hanan: crow.
③ Honghui: turtledove.
④ Hasha: the Yuanjiang River.

燕子九年不搬家，
旧家上面盖新房。
燕子欢喜地叫，
春耕的时间到了；
布谷欢喜地叫，
安排活计的日子来到。

万事万物醒了，
万事万物动了。
正月到，
男人爱想女人，
女人爱想男人；
家里的禽畜动起来了，
不动的没有了。
大公鸡冠子闪亮，
飞上屋顶啼叫，
忙爬粪塘糠堆去了；
鸭子扇起翅膀下水，
抬起头嘎嘎叫；
黄狗跳上蹦下，
使劲在灰地上扒窝；
小公猪东窜西窜，
一步不离跟母猪跑；
公羊晃动长角，
追逐母羊吃草；

did not move for nine years,
and built new houses on top of the old ones.
When swallows cried cheerfully,
It was time for spring ploughing;
when cuckoos cried cheerfully,
It was time to make arrangements for planting.

Everything woke up
and started to move around.
When January came,
men desire women,
and women, men;
The livestock at each household began to move around,
with no exception.
The big roosters with the shining crests
flew up to the roof to crow,
and then busied themselves with foraging the compost pit and bran piles;
the ducks flapped their wings and went into the water,
and quaked with their heads reaching up;
the yellow dogs jumped up and down,
trying to dig the dirt;
the little boars ran left and right,
following the sows closely;
the rams moved around with their long horns,
chasing the ewes and eating the grass;

马儿扬起鬃毛，
闪开四蹄撒欢；
水牛甩动尾巴，
在泥塘里打滚……

正月到，
山野的鸟兽动起来了：
松林鹧鸪飞，
草丛鹌鹑叫，
山上马鹿跃，
山坳草豹叫，
山沟野猪闹，
崖边麂子跳……

正月到，
水里的鱼虫动起来：
杂草下泥鳅摆尾，
浮萍下鱼儿翻起波浪，
泥塘里蚯蚓扭动腰肢，
田水中虾巴虫舞蹈。

正月到，
五谷子种动起来：
篾箩里的谷种伸腰，
豆荚里的豆种眨眼，
封火楼上芋头冒芽啧啧响。

the horses raised their manes,
running with their hoofs kicking to their delight;
the buffaloes flicked their tails,
wallowing in the mud pool...

When January came,
birds and animals in the mountains started to move around:
Partridges flew in the pine forest,
as quails cried in the grass,
red deer leaped in the mountains,
leopards cried in the valleys,
wild boars played in the gully
muntjacs jumped by the edge of the cliffs...

When January came,
fish and worms in the water started to move around:
loaches wagged their tails under the weeds,
as fish splashed the water under the duckweed,
earthworms wriggled their backs in the mud pond,
and the larvae of dragonflies danced in the paddy water.

When January came,
seeds of various grains started to grow:
the grain seeds in the bamboo baskets were stretching out,
as peas in the pods blinked their eyes,
the taros in the fireproof place sprouted.

燕子叫了，
春耕的时节来到；
布谷鸟叫了，
下种的时节来到。
挖田种地的人，
闲着的心痒起来了：
鸡肥要看好鸡种，
谷壮要靠好谷种，
筛子筛谷种，
簸箕簸谷种，
秕谷落下地，
谷种箩里装；
清水泡谷种，
瓦缸泡谷种，
鸡蛋献一个，
谷神来保佑。

小鸡要由母鸡抱，
谷种要用树叶捂。
哪样树叶才暖和？
宽厚的桅桐树叶最暖和。
采回桅桐叶，
背箩捂谷种，
冷水浇三次，
热水浇三回；
三天三夜盖被子，
根芽出来白生生。

When swallows cried,
it was the time for spring ploughing;
when cuckoos sang,
it was the time for sowing.
Those who farmed,
were ready to be busy again after the rest:
like fat chicken that depended on good breeds,
good rice depended on fine seeds.
The seeds were sieved with sieves
and winnowed with winnowing pans,
so that the shriveled seeds fell to the ground,
while the good ones were kept in the bamboo baskets.
The seeds were then soaked in clear water
and in vats.
And an egg was offered
to the god of cereals to bless the crops.

Like chicks who were hatched by the hens,
the grain seeds needed to be covered with leaves.
What leaves could keep them warm?
The broad Paulownia leaves were the best.
The leaves were collected
and used to cover the seeds in the bamboo baskets.
The seeds were watered with cold water three times
and then hot water three times;
after three days and nights under the quilt,
the seeds grew tender and white sprouts.

快整好寨脚的秧田，
谷种要叫阿爸了，
寨脚平滑的秧田阿爸等它；
谷种要叫阿妈了，
谷种要吃奶水了，
龙潭边的秧田阿妈来抱它。
背出谷种撒秧田，
上埂撒三把，
下埂撒三把，
中间撒三把；
撒谷种要像雨点一样均匀，
要像姑娘帽子上的银泡花。

谷种的奶汁是哪样？
龙潭里出来的清泉水。
看秧田要像照管娃娃，
不要让牛马鼠雀糟蹋，
一天要放三回水，
一天要洒三回水，
让谷种快快成长。

谷种撒下去，
大田要翻犁，
犁耙没有牛，
脚手粗壮难种田。

It was time to get ready the rice nursery paddy at the foot of the village.

The seeds like children would need to be parented,

and the flat and smooth paddy at the foot of the village was like their father;

the seeds would need to be nurtured like infants

with milk,

and the paddy by the Longtan spring embraced them like their mother.

The seeds were carried to the paddy and sown,

three handfuls to the upper field,

three to the lower field,

and three to the middle field.

The seeds should be sown as evenly as raindrops

or the silvery beads on girls' hats.

What was like milk to the rice seeds?

It was the clean spring water from the Longtan spring.

Watching over the nursery paddies were like taking care of infants,

lest cattle, horses, mice and birds may trample on them.

The paddies should be drained

and then irrigated three times every day

to help the seedlings grow quickly.

Now that the seeds had been sown,

the fields should be ploughed,

but without the cattle,

even strong arms and legs could hardly grow crops.

请问寨头的长老，
犁田的牛去哪里找？
犁田的牛松格①
这地方有，
买牛的银子要石头一样多。

身背晌午饭，
各去一条路，
买牛来到松格：
问水牛价钱值多少，
看水牛两角开不开②，
瞧水牛尾巴花不花③。

两只牛角如竹笋，
大弓一样朝里弯；
牛尾上下没有花，
犁田力气大，
一根索子拉着就会耙。
威咀看着会顺眼，
实车④望见会喜欢。
牛价不高把牛买，

---

① 松格：即今遮萨镇，在红河县境内。
② 按哈尼族相牛的经验，若两只牛角间距大，则说明这头牛力气小。
③ 哈尼族曾经认为，牛尾有花则不吉利。
④ 实车：哈尼族传说中管庄稼的神。

They asked the elders who lived at the entrance of the village
where to find the ploughing cattle,
the ploughing cattle could be found
in Songge①,
but it would take as many ingots of silver as stones everywhere.

Carrying the lunch,
the villagers went
to buy the cattle at Songge:
They asked for the price of the cattle,
checked how far apart the tips of the two horns were②,
and if the tail had split ends③.

The two horns were like the bamboo shoots,
bending towards each other like bows.
The tail had no split ends,
so the cattle was strong
and could plough with only one rope.
Weizu would be the looks of it,
and Shiche④ would be delighted on seeing it.
The price wasn't bad,

---

① Songge: Today's Yisa town, Honghe County.

② According to Hani's experience with cattle, the farther apart the two horns, the weaker the cattle.

③ The Hani people used to think that the split ends of cattle's tails meant bad luck.

④ Shiche: the god of crops according to Hani legends.

高高兴兴赶回家。
拉着牛回家的是哪个？
拉着牛回家的是跛脚里德。

松格梁子的牛在不惯高山，
买来几天就死了。
犁田耙田的尖角牛死了，
哈尼男人老实着急，
连续两天敬献威咀的饭，
问没有牛来犁田怎样栽；
连续两天敬献实车的饭，
问没有牛来耙田怎样种。

请问寨中的长老，
从松格买来的牛死了，
犁田耙田的牛哪里去找？
白宏①垤玛②有牛卖，
一头牛要两头牛的价钱，
买牛的银子要像石头一样多。

请问白宏垤玛的牛主人，
牛的价钱要多少？
牛身子多大，
不能要牛身子重的钱；
牛毛有多少根，

---

① 白宏：哈尼族的一个支系。
② 垤玛：地名，在红河县境内。

so they bought it and led it back to the village.
Who brought the cattle back?
It was Lide, the person who walked with a limp.

The cattle from the Songge ridge was not used to living in the high mountains
and died only a few days after it was bought.
With the pointed-horned ploughing cattle died,
Hani men were very worried,
and so they offered food to god Weizu two days in a row,
asking how to plough the fields without the cattle
and offered food to god Shiche two days in a row,
asking how to harrow the fields without the cattle.

They went to ask the elder living in the middle of the village
that since the cattle bought from Songge had died
where else they could find a ploughing cattle.
Cattle were sold in Zhima① by the Baihong② people,
but one was sold for the price of two
and so it would cost as many ingots of silver as stones everywhere.

They went to Zhima to ask the Baihong owner of the cattle,
how much the cattle was.
The weight of the cattle
should not be its price;
the number of its hairs

① Zhima: name of a place, in today's Honghe County.
② Baihong: a subgroup of the Hani people.

不能要牛毛一样多的钱。
买卖双方不吃亏，
牛价给你银子四五钱。

兑了银子买成牛，
拉着耕牛转回家；
吆喝耕牛快快走，
早早回家犁田耙田。

挖田的人，
四个眼的犁快安好，
九个齿的木耙快修理；
犁田要犁三回，
耙田要耙三道，
威咀吃的谷米要栽出来，
实车吃的谷米要栽出来。

布谷叫了，
春耕时节来到；
燕子叫了，
安排农活的时节来到。
田里的水一天比一天变热了，
男人女人赶快去下田。

众人：萨——萨！

二月

萨啦阿依——
旧的一月过去，

should not be its price.
To be fair to both the buyer and the seller,
the cattle should be priced at four or five qian of silvers.

They paid silver for the cattle,
and then pulled the cattle back home;
yelling at the cattle to move quickly
to be back early to plough and harrow the field.

Experienced farmers
quickly assembled the four-eyed plough
and repaired the nine-toothed wooden harrow:
the field would be ploughed three times
and then harrowed three times,
to grow the best rice for Fairy Weizu
and god Shiche.

When the cuckoos cried,
it was the time for the spring ploughing;
when the swallows sang,
it was the time to organize the farmwork.
The water in the field was getting warmer by the days,
so it was time for men or women to hurry to the fields.

Everyone: Sa—Sa!

February

Sala'ayi—
An old month had passed,

新的一月来到。
山上的桃花开了，
寨边的染饭花香了。
女人织布忙，
家家织布机“滴答”地响；
男人犁田不知太阳落山，
烧起篝火歇田房①。
不是过年的时候，
要染黄糯米过一回节。

高山上撒荞种的时节到了，
河坝里栽棉花的时节到了，
背肥的女人不歇脚，
像采花的蜜蜂出出进进；
割草的男人，
左手拿钩把②，
右手把弯刀紧紧地握，
砍倒刺丛杂草。
挖田的男人，
忙得淌汗的时节来到了：
一天干十天吃的日子，

① 歇田房：在田房里吃住。
② 钩把：砍草用的竹木工具。

and a new month had begun.

The peach trees in the mountains were in blossom,

and the butterflybush flowers by the village smelled sweet fragrance.

Women were busy with weaving,

looms "rap rap rap" was heard in every household;

men kept ploughing without noticing the sunset

and so built the bonfire and rested in the field shed①.

Even though it was not the new year,

glutinous rice was dyed yellow with butterflybush flower for celebration.

The time had come for sowing the buckwheat seeds in the mountains,

and for planting cotton on the riverbank.

Women who carried manure walked without stopping,

shuttling in and out like bees gathering honey;

men who cut the grass,

with bamboo hooks② in the left hand,

and the sickle tightly in the right,

cut down the thorny weeds;

men who dug the field

had entered the sweating season:

they consume ten days' calorie in doing one day's work.

---

① rested in the field shed: a shed for eating and staying in the field.

② bamboo hooks: a bamboo or wood tool for cutting grass.

挥动亮闪闪的大锄头，
泥水沾脸不怕，
挖断土狗蚯蚓的头不怕，
挖断泥鳅黄鳝的腰不怕；
你挖我不停，
我挖你不闲。

布谷鸟叫了，
春耕的时间来到；
燕子叫了，
催生产的日子来到；
汉人下种的季节到了，
哈尼栽秧的季节快来了。
寨边的小秧盖满秧田，
嫩汪汪像床缘行毯；
秧苗望着山下了，
等着要嫁大田了。
弟兄不分家会在一处，
谷秧不分家不会在一处。

众人：萨——萨！

三月

萨啦阿依——
旧的一月过去了，
新的一月来到。

Waving the big shiny hoes,

they didn't care mud splashed onto their faces,

were not afraid of cutting the heads of mole crickets and earthworms,

or of cutting the loaches and eels in half;

you dug, so did I,

and I dug, so did you.

When cuckoos cried,

it was the time for spring ploughing;

when swallows sang,

the planting was in full swing;

the Han people would sow the seeds,

while the Hani people would transplant the seedlings.

The nursery paddy by the village was covered with the seedlings,

like the soft blanket on a flatbed;

the seedlings looked down the mountain,

as if waiting to be betrothed to the fields.

Brothers who didn't part their ways stay together,

but seedlings that did not part their ways would not be together.

Everyone: SA—SA!

March

Sala'ayi—

An old month had passed,

and a new one had begun.

勤劳的伙子，
挖田地的男人，
快上山砍锥栗木，
修理九齿木耙；
快下箐扯老藤子，
扭成牢牢的耙索；
架起弯角的牯子牛，
耙田要耙三回，
一天干十天吃的日子，
吃奶的小牛叫娘不要心疼，
三岁的小牛上耙不要手软，
九岁的老牛上耙不要心软。

满月的小娃，
一天变一个样，
弟兄不分家会在一处，
秧田不分家不会在一处，
秧苗姑娘长大，
要嫁婆家了。
耙田过后三天，
欢欢喜喜开秧门。

勤劳的女人，
半夜起来烧火煮饭，
床上娃娃蹬开被窝忙不得看，
腰带散落地上顾不得管；
栽秧吃的饭菜煮好了，
公鸡还未跳出窝。

The hardworking lads,
the wild-vegetation digging and removing men,
all hurried up the mountains to cut the pyramidal chestnut wood,
to repair the nine-tooth harrow;
all hurried down the valley to cut the old rattan,
and to twist them into firm raking ropes.
They then made the cattle with the crooked horns
to draw the harrow to harrow the fields three times.
Each day they completed ten days' work,
not feeling bad when the suckling calf cried for its mom,
or afraid to fasten the harrow on the three-year old calf
or sorry to fasten it on the nine-year-old cattle.

A one-month old baby
looked different every day.
Brothers, not separated, lived together with their family,
but seedlings, not separated, would not.
Like young women, the seedlings had grown up,
and it was time for them to be married out.
Three days after the field was ploughed and harrowed,
the seedling transplanting began.

The hardworking women
got up at midnight to cook meals,
too busy to take care of the babies who had kicked off the cover
or the girdles that had fallen on the floor;
when the meals for seedling planters were ready,
the roosters had not come out of their nests.

栽秧要先栽三把，
不是我家先栽秧①，
不是我家后栽秧②。
先栽的头把秧，
是人的面份；
中间栽的第二把秧，
是庄稼的面份；
后栽的第三把秧，
是牛马牲畜的面份。

栽秧要用什么献？
要染黄糯米饭敬献，
要染红鸡蛋来敬献。
栽秧的日子，
田坝像赶街子一样热闹：
阿爸阿妈来栽秧，
兄弟姐妹来栽秧，
亲戚朋友来栽秧。

彝家栽秧的日子，
傣家栽秧的日子，
哈尼栽秧的日子，

① 哈尼族曾有最先栽秧不吉利的说法。
② 哈尼族认为，后栽秧是对神的不恭。

The first three handfuls of seedlings
had nothing to do with which family was the first①,
or the last②.
The first handful of the seedlings planted
was dedicated to all the people;
the second handful of seedlings planted,
was dedicated to all the crops;
the third handful of seedlings planted,
was dedicated to all the livestock.

What was offered as a sacrifice for the seedling-planting season?
They dyed glutinous rice yellow,
and eggs red.
On the seedling-planting days,
the rice paddies were as exciting as the fair:
papas and mamas coming to plant the seedlings,
brothers and sisters coming to plant the seedlings,
the relatives and friends coming to plant the seedlings.

On the days when the Yi people planted the seedlings,
on the days when the Dai people planted the seedlings,
on the days when the Hani people planted the seedlings,

---

① The Hani people used to think it unlucky to be the first to transplant seedlings.

② The Hani people think it disrespectful to the gods to be the last to transplant seedlings.

阿爸阿妈不要害羞，
哥哥姐姐不要害羞；
你栽秧我不歇手，
我栽秧你不闲着。
威咀吃的栽下了，
实车吃的栽下了，
一季栽秧一年粮。

众人：萨——萨！

四月

萨啦阿依——
旧的一月过去了，
新的一月来到。
梨树结出嫩嫩的绿果，
仰阿娜①的日子来到了。

低洼的地方有千百处，
最低的是河水淌的地方；
高高的山峰有千座万座，
最高的是孟资山②。
地上大大小小的动物出来游，
天上星星斗斗出来游，

---

① 仰阿娜：哈尼语，有休息之意。它是哈尼族支系叶车人的一种传统习俗，在每年农历四月水田栽插禾苗后举行。

② 孟资山：在红河县境内。

parents shouldn't be shy,
nor should brothers and sisters;
they all worked together without stop,
they all worked together without rest.
What was for Weizu was planted;
and what was for Shiche was planted;
and what was for people for the whole year was planted.

Everyone: Sa—Sa!

April

Sala'ayi—
An old month had passed,
and a new one had begun.
When the pear trees produced tender green fruits,
it was time for Yang'ana①.

There were hundreds and thousands of low places,
but the lowest was where rivers ran;
there were tens and thousands of mountains,
but the highest was the Mengzi Mountain②.
Animals of all sizes came out to roam the earth,
and stars of all kinds came out to roam the sky;

① Yang'ana: are transplanted. it has the connotation of rest in Hani. It is a tradition of the Yeche, a branch of the Hani people, to celebrated Yang'ana every lunar April after the seedlings are transplanted.

② Mengzi Mountain: in Honghe County.

山头的妥底玛依开放，
山沟的索都扎依①开放。
女人的包头角，
像老鹰翅膀晃动；
姑娘身上的腰带亮闪闪，
比妥底玛依还漂亮。

姑娘小伙仰阿娜，
老人小娃仰阿娜，
村村寨寨仰阿娜，
敲起牛皮鼓仰阿娜，
敲起铓锣仰阿娜；
不上山欢乐的人没有了，
脸上不见笑的人没有了。

古时候阿匹拾德棕莫②，
站在孟资山上，
一眼又一眼望下去，
傣家的坝子让它谷子好，
汉人的地方让它谷子好；
一眼又一眼朝上看去，
高山的荞子让它饱满，
五谷是让人不死的药。

---

① 索都扎依：一种山杜鹃花。
② 阿匹拾德棕莫：哈尼族传说中最先庆祝仰阿娜的女祖先。

the Todimayi on mountaintops were blossoming,
and the Suoduzhayi① in the valley were blossoming.
The women's scarfs
were like eagles' wings flapping in the air;
the girls' girdles were shiny,
more beautiful than the Todimayi.

Girls and lads celebrated Yang'ana,
the old and young celebrated Yang'ana,
all villages celebrated Yang'ana,
the cowhide drums were hit for Yang'ana,
and the gongs were struck for Yang'ana.
Not one wasn't up on the mountains to have fun
and no one had worries on their face.

In ancient times, Apishidezongmo②,
stood in the Mengzi Mountain,
enjoyed looking down at
the crops on the plain where the Dai people lived and blessed them
and the crops in the place where the Han people lived and blessed them;
she enjoyed looking up at
the buckwheat in the mountain and blessed them to be full.
She did all this because the cereals were the medicine that kept people alive.

---

① Suoduzhayi: a kind of azalea.

② Shidezongmo: the legendary first female ancestor who celebrated the Yang'ana festival.

四月到了，
田地等着要梳头了，
比哭阿妈①飞出来了，
安排女人来薅头道秧。
比哭阿妈住在哪里？
住在墨索②这地方。
它从远远的地方叫着来，
催促人们快薅秧。

家里的女人，
丢开吃奶的娃娃，
像鸭子一样钻进田里，
黑草要拔干净，
黄草要拔干净；
你薅秧我不歇手，
我薅秧你不闲着。

众人：萨——萨！

五月

萨啦阿依——
旧的一月过去了，
新的一月来到。

---

① 比哭阿妈：一种小鸟。
② 墨索：古地名，地址不详。

In April.
the fields were waiting to be combed,
and Biku'ama① flew out of the sky,
telling women it was time to weed the field for the first time.
Where did Biku'ama live?
It lived in Mosuo②.
It came from afar crying,
urging people to weed the field soon.

All the women
left behind their suckling babies
and went into the fields like ducks,
to weed the black weeds
and to weed the yellow weeds;
you were weeding, so did I,
and I was weeding, so did you.

Everyone: Sa—Sa!

May

Sala'ayi—
An old month had passed,
and a new one had begun.

---

① Biku'ama: a kind of small bird.
② Mosuo: name of an ancient place, whereabouts unknown.

雨水下地了，
竹笋节节冒土了。
一年不满过第三次年的日子来了，
矻扎①的时节来了。

威咀不请自己来，
实车不请自己来；
威咀要来看山寨，
实车要来保庄稼。
砍棵直直的松树安磨秋，
背来绿绿的松枝撒马路②，
好马忘不了走过的路，
哈尼人忘不了磨秋场。
七十岁的老人来了，
三岁的小娃来了，
小伙子一对对骑磨秋，
小姑娘一个一个荡秋千。

秋千高高地飞，
把病害甩开；
磨秋团团地转，

---

① 矻扎：哈尼族举行的一个盛大传统节日，节日期间人们骑磨秋、荡秋千。

② 松枝撒马路：表示迎接威咀神的意思。

The rainwater soaked the ground,
and the bamboo-shoots broke out of the ground section by section.
It was time for the third celebration of the year:
it was the season of Kuzha①.

Weizu needed no invitation,
nor did Shiche;
Weizu came to protect the village,
and Shiche came to protect the crops.
A straight pine tree was cut to make the Moqiu,
and the green pine branches were scattered on the road②,
Just as a good horse wouldn't forget the roads it walked,
the Hani people wouldn't forget the Moqiu playground.
Elderlies in their seventies came,
and children of three years of age came.
Young lads rode Moqiu in pairs (seesaw, Hani style)
and girls played on the swings one by one.

The swing flew high,
shaking the diseases off;
the Moqiu turned around,

---

① Kuzha: a grand traditional festival of the Hani people, where the most characteristic activities were the seesaw- and swing-playing (磨秋: Hani style seesaw).

② scatter pine branches on the road to welcome god Weizu.

把魔鬼撵走；
男人女人平平安安，
大寨小寨热热闹闹。

放倒磨秋吹热风，
水田要薅第二道草。
薅红草不留根，
薅黑草不留根；
看见秧苗绿油油，
家家户户心喜欢。

众人：萨——萨！

六月

萨啦阿依——
旧的一月过去了，
新的一月来到。
树林里达休①鸣叫了，
秧棵的肚子圆圆打苞了。
雷，你不要打，
雨，你不要下，
风，你不要刮，
让秧棵平安生长。

家里的男人，
不要四处窜玩，

① 达休：蝉。

driving the devils away.
Men and women were all safe and sound,
Villages, big or small, were all exciting and lively.

When Moqiu was put away, the blowing wind was warm,
and the rice paddies needed to be weeded a second time.
The red weeds were uprooted,
and the black ones, too;
seeing the green rice seedlings,
every family was delighted.

Everyone: Sa—Sa!

June

Sala'ayi—
An old month had passed,
and a new one had begun.
The Daxiu in forest chirped①,
and the rice seedlings produced full ear-shoots.
Please thunder not to rumble;
rain, not to fall;
and wind, not to blow.
The crops would be left to grow in peace.

All the men
were not idle;

---

① Daxiu: cicada.

快磨亮割草刀，
去砍净田边的杂草；
快扛起锄头，
去把田埂铲光滑。
铲下杂草埋肥料，
老鼠不敢来做窝，
害虫不敢来吃秧；
杀只小鸡祭谷神，
谷神长在秧苗旺。

众人：萨——萨！

七月

萨啦阿依——
旧的一月过去了，
新的一月来到。
七月吹热风，
谷子抽穗谷花香；
达休处处叫，
一年的粮挂到嘴边了。

勤劳的男人，
快拿起七尺长的竹刀，
砍倒田埂上的茅草；
快去砍来木条子，
修理漏雨的田房。

they quickly sharpened the sickles
to sythe the weeds by the fields;
they quickly picked up the hoes
to get ready the ridges in the fields.
They fertilized the newly weeded land
to deter the mice from nesting there
and pests from damaging the rice plants;
they killed a chick to make a sacrifice to the god of cereals,
the god of cereals that blessed the rice to be strong.

Everyone: Sa—Sa!

July

Sala'ayi—
An old month had passed,
and a new one had begun.
The wind in July was warm,
time for the rice ears to mature with their fragrance wafting in the air;
the chirping cicadas were heard everywhere,
and a year's grains were getting ever so closer to the mouth.

The hardworking men,
quickly picked up the seven-foot bamboo knifes
and cut down the thatches on the ridges;
they also got the timber
to fix the leaking field shed.

七月吃新谷①
的节气来到了，
挖来甜甜的竹笋，
摘来嫩嫩的豆荚，
炸出白生生的米花，
再祭一次谷神。

雷不要惊跑谷魂，
雨不要冲走谷魂，
风不要吹散谷魂；
愿谷子的脸转向寨子，
望着哈尼的大门。

众人：萨——萨！

八月

萨啦阿依——
旧的一月过去了，
新的一月来到。
达休不停地叫，
达休催秋收的时节到了。

谷穗弯腰了，
谷子要回家。
勤劳的男人，
快把打谷船②收好，

① 吃新谷：哈尼族的一个传统节日。
② 打谷船：打谷子的用具，形如船状。

July was the time for
the Chixingu festival①
The sweet bamboo shoots were dug,
and the tender pods were picked.
The white pop-rice
was offered as a sacrifice to the god of cereals one more time.

Please thunder, not to scare away the spirit of the rice,
and rain, not to wash away the spirit of the rice,
and wind, not to blow away the spirit of the rice.
Please rice, turn to the village
and look at the Hani's big gate.

Everyone: Sa—Sa!

August

Sala'ayi—
An old month had passed,
and a new one had begun.
Cicadas chirped without stop,
reminding people that it was time for the autumn harvest.

The ears of the rice were bending the plants,
and the rice was ready to be taken home.
The hardworking men
got the boat-shaped threshers② ready

---

① Chixingu: eating newly-harvested rice, a traditional Hani festival.

② boat-shaped thresher: a tool for threshing unhusked rice, shaped like a boat.

沟上的木桥要加固，
进村的大路要修宽；
勤劳的女人，
快缝补装粮的麻袋，
快准备割谷的锯镰。

栽在河坝的棉花开了，
快背上布包拾棉花；
种在山梁上的高粱红了，
快背着背篓去采；
梯田里的谷子黄了，
汗水淌出来的粮食到口了，
哈尼像蜜蜂一样忙的日子来了！

锯镰快快割，
谷船重重打，
你割谷我不歇手，
我打谷你不松闲；
庄稼收到家，
杀一只母鸡，
杀一只公鸡，
蒸一甑糯米饭，
祭献守仓的谷神。

众人：萨——萨！

九月

萨啦阿依——

reinforced the wooden bridge over the stream,
and widened the main road into the village;
the hardworking women
quickly sewed the rice sacks
and readied the harvesting sickles.

The cotton on the riverbank was ripe,
so they hurried to pick the cotton carrying their cloth bags;
the sorghum on the ridge turned red,
so they hurried to harvest it carrying their bamboo baskets;
the rice in the terraced rice paddies became yellow,
so the grains, watered with their sweat, were now ready:
the bee-like busy time had arrived!

The sickles were cutting quickly,
and threshers were beating heavily.
You were harvesting, so was I,
and I was threshing, so were you.
Now that the rice was taken home,
they first killed a hen
and a rooster.
and cooked a steamer of glutinous rice
to offer a sacrifice to the god of cereals who guarded barns.

Everyone: Sa—Sa!

September

Sala'ayi—

旧的一月过去了，
新的一月来到。
样样庄稼收回来了，
家里粮仓满满的了。

勤劳的人，
吃着新米要想着明年。
锄头要加钢
趁天热好挖田；
你挖我不歇手，
我挖你不松闲。
搭好骡子背一样的埂子，
挖过头道田，
哈尼要过十月年。

众人：萨——萨！

十月

萨啦阿依——
旧的一年过去了，
新的一年来到。
最后的一日翻过来了，
最后的一月翻过来了。
住河坝的傣家，
有自己过年的日子，
住大寨子的汉人，
有自己过年的日子；
不是山上的树没有脚，

An old month had passed,
and a new one had begun.
Crops of all kinds had been harvested and taken home,
filling all the barns full.

The hardworking men
tasted the new rice but were preparing for the next year.
The hoes should be processed to have more steel in it,
so that the fields could be dug while it was still warm;
you dug, so did I,
and I dug, so did you.
They then built in the field the walk-paths like the mule's back.
After they dug field the first time,
the Hani people were ready to celebrate the New Year in October.

Everyone: Sa—Sa!

October

Sala'ayi—
An old month had passed,
and a new one had begun.
The last day of a year had passed,
so did the the last month of a year.
The Dai people who lived on the riverbank,
had their day of the New Year;
the Han people who lived in big villages
had their day of the New Year;
Unlike those trees in the mountains that couldn't move around,

哈尼也有过年的时候。
哈尼的年哪时过？
年头年尾怎样分？
哈尼过年在十月间①，
吃新谷饭的那天算一年。

最先吃年饭的是哪个？
最先吃年饭的是腊咪阿母②。
最先踩粑粑的是哪个？
最先踩粑粑的是欧红然依③。
叶车④最先煮年饭的是哪个？
是火白火谷⑤阿妈。

花开有最好的一朵，
一日有最好的时辰。
哈尼过年哪天日子好？
属兔的日子最好；
天神保平安，
地神保平安，

---

① 哈尼族将十月定为岁首，十月年，是哈尼族最盛大的节日。
② 腊咪阿母：哈尼族传说中的一个女祖先。
③ 欧红然依：哈尼族传说中的一个女祖先。
④ 叶车：哈尼族的一个支系。
⑤ 火白火谷：哈尼族传说中的一个女祖先。

the Hani people also had their day of the New Year.
When did the Hani people celebrate the New Year?
When was the beginning and when was the end of the year?
the Hani people celebrated the New Year in October①,
and the day they ate the newly-harvested rice was the end of the year.

Who was the first to eat the New Year's meal?
Lami Amu② was the first to eat the New Year meal.
Who was the first to make the glutinous rice cake?
Ouhong Ranyi③ was the first to make it.
Who was the first to cook the New Year's meal in Yeche④?
It was mother Huobai Huogu⑤.

There is the most beautiful flower among all flowers
and there is the best hour of all the hours of a day.
Which day is the best for the Hani people to celebrate the New Year?
the day of the rabbit is the best;
God of heaven please keep us safe;
god of earth please keep us safe;

---

① The Hani set October as the beginning of a year; the New Year in October is the Hani's grandest festival.

② Lami Amu: a female ancestor in Hani legends.

③ Ouhong Ranyi: a female ancestor in Hani legends.

④ Yeche: one branch of the Hani nationality with only one person.

⑤ Huobai Huogu: a female ancestor in Hani legends.

寨神保平安，
寨寨热热闹闹，
家家喜喜欢欢。

众人：萨——萨！

guardian of the village please keep us safe,
so that all the villages are lively,
and all the families are joyful.

Everyone: Sa—Sa!